# William—The Gangster

1. Just—William
2. More—William
3. William Again
4. William—The Fourth
5. Still—William
6. William—The Conqueror
7. William—The Outlaw
8. William—In Trouble
9. William—The Good
10. William
11. William the Bad
12. William's Happy Days
13. William's Crowded Hours
14. William—The Pirate
15. William—The Rebel
16. William—The Gangster
17. William—The Detective
18. Sweet William
19. William—The Showman
20. William—The Dictator
21. William and Air Raid Precautions
22. William and the Evacuees
23. William Does His Bit
24. William Carries On
25. William and the Brains Trust
26. Just William's Luck
27. William—The Bold
28. William and the Tramp
29. William and the Moon Rocket
30. William and the Space Animal
31. William's Television Show
32. William—The Explorer
33. William's Treasure Trove
34. William and the Witch
35. William and the Pop Singers
36. William and the Masked Ranger
37. William the Superman
38. William the Lawless

*Just – William* a facsimile of the first (1922) edition
*Just William – As Seen on TV*
*More Just William – As Seen on TV*
*William at War*
*Just William at Christmas*
*Just William on Holiday*
*Just William at School*
*Just William Through the Ages*

"OH, IT'S GUY FAWKES' DAY!" SAID THE LITTLE GIRL. "ARE
YOU HAVING FIREWORKS? HOW EXCITING! MAY I COME?"

*(See page 183)*

# William—The Gangster

RICHMAL CROMPTON

Illustrated by Thomas Henry

MACMILLAN CHILDREN'S BOOKS

THIS BOOK IS DEDICATED

TO MY NIECE

# MARGARET DISHER

WITH LOVE

First published 1934

First published in this edition 1985 by
Pan Macmillan Children's Books
This edition reprinted 1995 by
Macmillan Children's Books
A division of Macmillan Publishers Limited
25 Eccleston Place, London SW1W 9NF
Basingstoke and Oxford
www.macmillan.co.uk
Associated companies throughout the world

5 7 9 8 6

British Library Cataloguing in Publication Data
Crompton, Richmal
    William–the gangster.
    Rn: Richmal Crompton Lamburn    I. Title
    823'.912[J]    PZ7
ISBN: 0-333-38906-9

Printed and bound in Great Britain by
Mackays of Chatham plc, Kent

# Contents

# An invitation from William

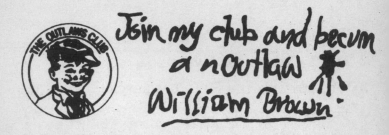

*Join my club and becum a n Outlaw*
*William Brown*

# You can join the Outlaws Club!

You will receive
**a special Outlaws wallet containing**
your own Outlaws badge
the Club Rules
a pad for secret messages
*and*
a letter from William giving you
the secret password

To join, send a postal order for £2.50 and a letter
telling us you want to join the Outlaws, with your
name and address written in block capitals, to:

**The Outlaws Club**
**Macmillan Children's Books**
**25 Eccleston Place**
**London SW1W 9NF**

You must live in the United Kingdom or the
Republic of Ireland in order to join.

# Chapter 1

# William—The Gangster

William and the Outlaws, with a handful of their
followers, wandered disconsolately down the road,
carrying a large garden syringe. The garden syringe was
filled with water, but was evidently in bad repair, for it
shed an ample stream of its contents on the ground as
they walked. William stopped anxiously to inspect it.

"There'll be none left in a minute," he prophesied
gloomily, "an' we're sure to meet them as soon as it's
empty."

Almost immediately came a rustle in the hedge,
followed by a hail of missiles—peas from pea-shooters,
stones from catapults, spurts of water from water-
pistols. The Outlaws raised their cumbersome weapon
and levelled it at the hidden foes, but already most of the
contents had leaked out, and when the handle was
finally pushed home only the faintest trickle emerged
and fell harmlessly on to the dust at their feet. The
ambush leapt out of the hedge with a shout of triumph
and fell upon the Outlaws. The Outlaws and their
followers made a spirited resistance, but the artillery of
pea-shooters and catapults and water-pistols kept up a
relentless fire. In the end they betook themselves
ignominiously to flight, closely followed by their foes.

Hardly had they shaken off their pursuers and were
making their way across country to the old barn, when
they were set upon by a second lot of boys, also armed

with water-pistols, catapults, pea-shooters, and, in addition, an air-gun that discharged corks with unerring aim and painful violence. Once more the Outlaws and their supporters put up a plucky but unavailing struggle before, blinded by water-pistols and bruised by stones and corks, they turned to flee.

They reached the old barn battered and breathless, William still carrying the garden syringe. He put it down on the ground and looked at it dispassionately.

"It's absolutely no good at all," he said.

"'Course it isn't," said Ginger dejectedly. "They wouldn't have given it us if it had worked."

Douglas was wiping the water from his eyes.

"I couldn't see half the time," he said. "They kept getting me with water-pistols. The first lot was Hubert Lane's gang, wasn't it?"

"Yes, and the second Bertie Franks's."

"We'll have to *do* something," said William. "We can't go on like this."

"Yes, but what can we do?" asked Ginger simply.

They gazed at each other in silence.

The irony of the situation was that the fashion of armed gangs carrying on guerilla warfare against their foes had been originated by William himself. William had been given an air-gun by an unusually understanding uncle. He had bought a water-pistol with an unexpected tip, Ginger had contributed a catapult, and Douglas another air-gun. Thus equipped they had gathered together their followers and sallied forth to do battle with their enemies. Meeting Hubert Lane in the village, surrounded by a bodyguard of cronies, they had attacked and put them to flight with the greatest ease. Flushed with success, they had later attacked them again with the same gratifying results. But in the meantime Hubert Lane had been doing some thinking, and the

"IT'S ABSOLUTELY NO GOOD AT ALL," WILLIAM DECLARED.

results of his thinking appeared the next day in the shape of water-pistols, catapults, and pea-shooters, with which he had armed his followers. Moreover, he increased the numbers of his followers by the simple expedient of paying them a penny a day each for following him. But still, though outnumbered, the Outlaws remained victorious. They were nimble in dodging, brisk in firing, courageous in personal encounter.

The situation was next complicated by the action of Bertie Franks, who usually constituted himself Hubert Lane's lieutenant. He had grown tired of a subordinate position and had set up as head of a gang himself, taking with him many of Hubert's followers. He paid his followers a halfpenny a day, but occasionally doled out a ration of cream-buns, so that on the whole their followers were about equal in number.

The three gangs attacked each other indiscriminately whenever they met, and the Outlaws held their own easily even against both hostile gangs combined—till the catastrophe happened. The catastrophe was the confiscation of all their weapons by William's father after a practice in the back garden, during which two windows were broken and Mr. Brown himself, coming to investigate the matter, received in his face the entire contents of a water-pistol discharged by William and intended for Ginger.

Not only were the weapons confiscated, but William's pocket-money was forfeited for an indefinite period in order to pay for the windows. Weaponless, the Outlaws knew that it would be impossible to face their foes with any hope of victory. In vain they searched for fresh weapons. The only one they could find was the garden syringe presented to Ginger by his father's gardener because it leaked so badly as to be useless for gardening purposes. It proved, of course, to be equally useless as a weapon of offence, but the Outlaws clung to it with a pathetic hope that one day they would meet their enemies before the contents had entirely oozed away.

"It's better than nothin'," said Douglas. "I mean, it holds a jolly lot of water."

"Yes," objected Ginger, "but only for about two minutes, an' it's an awful nuisance having to hold it when you're fighting. You can't even hit anyone with it 'cause the handle comes off."

"Well, we jolly well can't go on like this," said William again decisively.

The others looked at him with that mixture of hopefulness and resentment with which one looks at one's chief when things are going badly.

"You said that before," said Ginger, "but what're we goin' to *do* about it?"

William, who had not led the Outlaws all these years without acquiring something of the finesse that marks the true leader of men, shifted the conversation to another angle.

"Well, it's jus' about tea-time," he said, "an' I'm goin' home. There's strawberry jelly an' I'm jolly well not goin' to miss it."

There followed, as he knew there would, an animated discussion on the rival claims of different flavours in jelly, Ginger hotly declaring himself in favour of raspberry, Douglas in favour of greengage, and the others in favour of vanilla, gooseberry, strawberry, banana, and apricot.

Under cover of the general argument William made good his escape.

He walked home slowly—for the enemy gangs, too, would now be at tea or on their way to tea—and thoughtfully—for he realised that his prestige was at stake. It was up to him, as leader of the gang, to extricate his followers from the morass in which they had been landed.

His mother was entertaining a visitor in the drawingroom, and tea was laid for him alone on the dining-room table. So absorbed was he in the problems that confronted him that he did less than justice to the strawberry jelly, leaving quite a fair portion of it still adhering to the dish when he rose from the table. Then he made his way into the drawing-room and discovered that his mother's visitor was the Vicar's wife, a fact that increased his depression, for relations between him and the Vicar's wife were not cordial.

He sat down on a chair by the door and fixed a stony stare on her, hoping that his presence would hasten her departure and that then he could tackle his mother once again on the subject of the confiscated weapons. He had no real hope that anything would come of this, but he thought that he might as well try it.

The Vicar's wife, however, remained proof against the stony stare and continued to talk to Mrs. Brown. At first William, engaged in intensifying the stoniness of his stare till it reached a glassy imbecility, did not notice what she was talking about. Even when he realised that she was explaining her plans for forming a local branch of the League of Nations Union, the words conveyed nothing to him. She went on to talk about disarmament. The word disarmament again held no meaning for William, but a casual sentence attracted his attention.

"We want everyone in the world," she said, "to give up their arms and weapons of warfare."

"Yes," said William earnestly, caressing a bruise made by an especially large stone discharged from Hubert Lane's catapult. "Yes, that would be a *jolly* good thing."

The Vicar's wife gazed at him, surprised. How difficult it was, after all, she thought, to understand the child mind. And how often one misjudged through lack of understanding. Here, beneath this child's crude, noisy exterior, lay beauties of soul one had not suspected.

"You love peace, dear?" she said to William.

"Yes," said William feelingly. "I think it would be a jolly good idea if everyone had to give up their weapons. We'd get a bit of peace then."

"You see," said the Vicar's wife, turning to Mrs. Brown with shining eyes, "even a little child . . . "

But Mrs. Brown, though willing as his mother to give

William credit for almost any other virtue, jibbed at attributing to him a love of peace.

"*William!*" she said reproachfully. "And you fighting with those dreadful gangs all over the village!"

"I know," agreed William, "but that was before I heard her talking about peace and suchlike."

The Vicar's wife smiled at him fondly and once more thought how easy it was to misjudge people, especially children. Here she had been expending all her eloquence trying to persuade Mrs. Brown to join the new local branch of the League of Nations Union and wishing that that dreadful child would stop staring at her, and all the time it was in the child's mind that her words were finding soil and taking root and already even bearing fruit.

"Gangs, dear boy?" she said. "Tell me, what gangs?"

Mrs. Brown answered for him.

"They've got gangs, and they fight each other whenever they meet, and the mess they make of their clothes is simply *dreadful*."

William realised from her tone that an appeal to her to use her influence with his father for the return of the forfeited weapons would be useless. Another plan, however, was fast forming itself in his mind.

"But how *shocking*!" said the Vicar's wife, deeply distressed.

"Yes, I think so too, now," said William unctuously. "Now I've heard you talking about peace an' suchlike, I think so too."

A far-away look had come into the face of the Vicar's wife, a determined gleam into her eye.

"Dear boy," she said, "now that you see how wrong it all is, you must try to teach others, mustn't you?"

She paused thoughtfully. The light in her eye gleamed

yet more determinedly.

"I know, dear boy! We'll form a junior branch of the League of Nations Union, and *you* shall be its president. You and I will work together for peace. We will hold the inaugural meeting of it just before the inaugural meeting of the senior branch to which your mother is going to belong." Mrs. Brown opened her mouth to protest, then yielded to the inevitable and closed it again. "It will be an inspiration and example to us all. Think of that, dear boy."

William thought of it, and a strange smile flickered for a moment over his freckled countenance.

"Well, I must go and make the arrangements," said the Vicar's wife, rising briskly. "*Good*-bye, Mrs. Brown. Thank you so much for promising to join the branch. *Good*-bye, dear boy."

She described the incident to the Vicar as soon as she got home.

"William Brown?" said the Vicar. "I must say I'm surprised, dear. He's such a rough boy."

"Rough, yes," said the Vicar's wife, and continued with great fervour, but with a slight mixture of metaphors: "A rough diamond trailing clouds of glory."

Invitations to attend a meeting for the inauguration of a junior branch of the League of Nations Union were issued to the juvenile population of the village. There was no mention of disarmament—a word which in any case would have conveyed little or nothing to the minds of the recipients.

It was William who spread the rumour of a sumptuous tea to be given at the close of the meeting. The rumour grew till the promised tea assumed the proportions of a gargantuan feast—with jellies and blancmange and ices and cream-buns and doughnuts and chocolate biscuits and crackers and lemonade. But it was not solely this that induced every member of the gangs of Hubert Lane and Bertie Franks to accept the invitation. It was the prospect of falling upon the Outlaw's gang on the way home and finally demolishing it. The Outlaws' nimbleness and knowledge of circuitous routes would enable them to reach the Vicarage in safety, but, going away from it in the very presence of their foes, they would have no hope of escape.

Hubert Lane and Bertie Franks had made a truce over the matter. The Outlaws were to be surrounded with no chance of flight and utterly and ingloriously routed. Each member of the gangs was to bring his weapon to the meeting, suitably concealed on his person.

The day of the meeting arrived, and the Vicar's wife was pleased to see so large an attendance of children. She made a short opening speech in which she proposed, seconded, and elected William to be president of the branch. The others made no objection. Being president, their expressions said, would not save him from what was coming to him. They grimaced at each other in anticipatory delight.

William arose to make his presidential address.

"What I think is," he said earnestly, "that weapons of war and suchlike is all wrong. We ought to give 'em up an' live in peace an' so on like what she's jus' told us. An' what I think we oughter do is to give up all our weapons of war to her, so's we won't be able to use them any more even if we want to. I'll start by givin' up ours. Fetch it out, Ginger."

Ginger arose from the back of the hall and stepped forward bearing the impressive though useless garden syringe. Solemnly he laid it on the table in front of the Vicar's wife. She gazed at it in horror.

"But—*surely*," she said, "you don't mean to tell me that you use *that* to fight with?"

"We did," admitted William, "till you talked to us about peace an' not havin' weapons of war an' suchlike."

The Vicar's wife, deeply touched, turned to the audience.

"I'm sure, boys," she said, "that you will all follow this dear child's example and give up any such horrible weapons as you may have brought with you, and live in peace and harmony with each other for the future. . . . Will you come up one by one and give up anything of the

"HE'S GOT A WATER-PISTOL IN ONE POCKET AN' A CATAPULT IN THE OTHER," SAID WILLIAM, THE ACCUSER.

sort you may have with you?"

"I'll call out the names, shall I?" said William, and, with a gleam in his eye that was anything but pacific, announced: "Hubert Lane."

Hubert Lane was taken by surprise. So commanding was William's voice, so determined the eye of the

THE MEMBERS OF HUBERT'S GANG BEGAN TO LOOK ALARMED AND GUILTY.

Vicar's wife, that before he knew what he was doing he had advanced to the table. William's keen eye ran over his anatomy.

"He's got a water-pistol in that pocket an' a catapult in that," he said shortly.

"Give them up, dear boy," cooed the Vicar's wife. "Follow your little president's example and give them up. Put them here."

Bewildered and half hypnotised, Hubert Lane placed his weapons of war on the table in front of the Vicar's wife.

"Bertie Franks," called William.

Bertie Franks got up, sat down, got up again, and slowly approached the table. Again William's keen eye searched out the hiding-places of his weapons.

"He's got a pea-shooter in that pocket," he announced, "and a catapult up his sleeve."

"Give them up, dear boy," pleaded the Vicar's wife once more.

William, perceiving signs of reluctance if not actual objection on Bertie's countenance, snatched the weapons from their hiding-places himself before Bertie realised what he was doing.

"Thank you, dear boy," said the Vicar's wife suavely.

Blinking, Bertie returned to his seat. The rest was easy. The members of the gangs, called up one by one by William, followed their leaders' example like sheep. None made the slightest objection. In a few moments the table in front of the Vicar's wife was covered with a motley array of water-pistols, air-guns, catapults, and pea-shooters. Hubert Lane and Bertie Franks stared at it, open mouthed with dismay.

"Now, dear boys," said the Vicar's wife, flushed with pride at her achievement, "let us end our disarmament conference by securely locking up these weapons so that none of you will be tempted ever to use them again. . . . "

Hubert Lane suddenly recovered the power of speech.

"What about the tea?" he demanded.

"What tea?" said the Vicar's wife coldly.

"I thought there was going to be tea," persisted Hubert.

"*Certainly* not," said the Vicar's wife, still more coldly. "Our thoughts are—or should be—on higher things than tea. I'm afraid you're a very greedy little boy. . . . Come along, children."

She gathered up an armful of weapons, gave the rest to William to carry, and swept into the Vicar's study followed by the unwilling pacifists. In the study she opened an oak chest that stood just beneath the window, emptied the weapons into it from her arms and William's, shut it, locked it, and put the key into her pocket.

The members of the disarmament conference stood round, gazing with agonized eyes at the chest that concealed their treasures.

"Now run away, dear children," said the Vicar's wife briskly. "I must attend the senior branch meeting next. You may be sure that I shall tell them of the wonderful start made by the junior branch. Out of the mouths of babes and sucklings, you know. . . . Now I really mustn't dawdle here any longer."

She shooed the reluctant babes and sucklings out on to the lawn, and herself hurried round to the parish room, where a few sheepish grown-ups were awaiting her. The junior branch of the League of Nations Union stood in huddled, suspicious groups on the lawn, obviously unwilling to leave the premises unarmed and un-protected.

Suddenly William saw the Vicar approaching from the

direction of the church, a pile of Prayer Books in his arms.

He walked across the lawn to the french window that led into the study. William, seeing a chance of re-entering the room that held now all the armaments of the countryside, leapt forward to help him.

"Let me take some," he said courteously.

The Vicar looked at him vaguely.

"They want rebinding," he said. "Really, people are very careless. I can't think what they do with them. I'm always sending Prayer Books and hymn-books to be rebound. They'd last for *years* if only people would treat them properly." He glanced round the room. "I can't send them off till the end of the week. Now, where can I put them till then?"

Certainly there seemed little enough room to put anything. Every available space was full to overflowing of books, papers, pamphlets, and ledgers.

William's eyes wandered to the chest just beneath the window.

"Why not put them in that box?" he said innocently.

The Vicar brightened.

"Yes, yes," he said. "A splendid idea. I believe there's room for them in there. . . . "

"I'll go'n' ask for the key, shall I?" suggested William.

"No, no. I have a key," said the Vicar, burrowing in a pocket and finally bringing out a key-ring. "Let me see. . . . Yes, here it is. . . . Yes, I think it's an excellent place to keep the Prayer Books. . . . "

He bent down, unlocked the chest and opened it. A blank look came into his face as he gazed down at the contents.

"Dear, dear!" he said. "What's all this? Where have all these things come from? Pistols . . . " His bewilder-

ment disappeared as he remembered a play given by the
village dramatic society the week before in which pistols
had been freely used, and a frown of annoyance took its
place.

"Dear, dear! These should be in the acting-cupboard
in the Village Hall. How I wish people would put things
back into their proper places . . . !"

"Shall I take them?" said William eagerly.

"Yes, yes . . . I'd be very glad if you would. And I'll
speak to the secretary of the dramatic society about it.
The big cupboard on the right as you go into the Village
Hall. The key's at the shop next door, you know. . . . "

With almost incredible speed William gathered up the
pistols, air-guns, pea-shooters, catapults, and other
weapons. The Vicar watched him approvingly. He
remembered his wife saying just recently that they had
misjudged William Brown. She was certainly right. No
one could have been more helpful than he had been over
the matter of the hymn-books and acting properties.

"Put them tidily in the cupboard, my boy, and take
the key back to the shop when you've done it," he
called, as William vanished through the french window.
Then he settled down at his desk and, lost completely to
the world around him, began to prepare his annual
address to the Bee-keepers' Guild.

Meantime, in the parish room, the Vicar's wife was
addressing the inaugural meeting of the senior branch of
the League of Nations Union. The parish room was a
large room built on to the Vicarage, whose windows
looked out on to the Vicarage garden.

The Vicar's wife stood facing her audience with her
back to the window.

"And I want to tell you something," she was saying,
"that is of very good omen for the future of our branch. I
have just held the first meeting of our junior branch, and

those dear children have, in the cause of peace, given up all the horrible weapons against each other that they have been using, and from now on are determined to live together like little brothers."

On the lawn outside the window appeared a struggling mass of children. William had hastily distributed the weapons to his waiting gang, and they had fallen summarily upon their foes. Some were engaged in hand-to-hand struggles, others were discharging water pistols, catapults, and pea-shooters.

The audience stared, open eyed and open mouthed, at this amazing sight. The Vicar's wife, who was more than slightly deaf, did not even turn her head.

"And now that those dear children are setting us such a wonderful example of peace and goodwill," she went on, "I think that we ought to follow it and, like them, do our bit for the peace of the world."

The fight raged more furiously outside. Ginger had got Hubert Lane down in the middle of the rose-bed and was stuffing garden soil into his mouth. Bertie Franks, temporarily winded by his own water-pistol, and blinded by a cork discharged from his own air-gun, was trying ineffectively to take refuge up a copper beech. The whole garden was full of struggling, pummelling, wrestling, punching, catapulting, pea-shooting, water-shooting boys. The audience stared at the sight, paralysed by amazement. The Vicar's wife continued her impassioned exhortation.

"Rough and uncouth as those children are, there is in their hearts a real love of peace that should put us older people to shame."

The fight waxed yet more fierce, then became an inglorious rout, as Hubert Lane and Bertie Franks and their gangs turned to flee in wild disorder, closely pursued by the Outlaws' gang flourishing their weapons.

It was at this point that the Vicar's wife became aware of the glassy stare that her audience kept fixed upon the garden outside. She turned round, wondering if anything of an unusual nature could be happening in the garden to account for it. . . . No, the garden was empty. It looked a little untidy perhaps. She must speak to the gardener about letting it get so untidy. But there was nothing in it to cause any interest. The tense expressions of her audience must be due to her own eloquence. They were feeling, as indeed they well might feel, deeply moved.

"So what I beg and implore of you," she said, "is to follow those dear children's example and throw your whole energy into working for the peace of the world."

Her audience continued to gaze blankly at her.

# Chapter 2

# Three Cheers for Sweetikins

"Well, what shall we do with it?" said William. "It" was the half-holiday—an oasis in the desert of the school week—that was to take place to-morrow.

The Outlaws knitted their brows in speculation.

"Let's go skatin'," suggested Ginger, with a vague idea of being original.

"We can't," said William. "There isn't any ice."

"It might freeze in the night."

"Well, you couldn't skate, even if it did. You can't skate."

"How do you know I can't skate? I've never really tried. I might be able to skate if I tried. It's always begun to thaw before anyone would lend me their skates."

"Well, it would again, and, anyway, it's not going to freeze. It's quite warm."

"Then you suggest something if you won't listen to anything I say."

"All right. Let's go explorin'."

"How can we? We know all the country round here for miles an' *miles*."

"No, we don't—not really know it. I bet there's lots of the woods we don't know an' we might find *anythin'*. I shan't be surprised if we find wild animals and savages that no one's discovered because they've not looked hard enough."

The Outlaws did not seriously believe this, but the idea lent a certain glamour to the expedition, and, as no one had anything better to suggest, they agreed to devote the half-holiday to a thorough exploration of the woods of the neighbourhood.

But directly after lunch Ginger came to William's house, wearing a mournful expression.

"I say," he said, "my aunt that's staying with us wants us to take out her dog with us."

"Well, that'll be all right," said William. "Jumble's coming, anyway, an' another dog'll be fun."

But Ginger's gloom did not lighten.

"Not her dog," he said. "*Her* dog's no fun. It's not what you mean when you say a *dog*. It sits on a cushion an' eats all day an' snaps at anyone that goes near it. She's had the vet to it, and he says that it needs more exercise. So that's why she wants us to take it out. It'll be an awful nuisance."

"Well, let's not take it, then," said William. "She can't make us. There's no lor that you've got to take out other people's dogs whether you want to or not. We'll slip out before she's got it ready."

"Y-yes," said Ginger thoughtfully, "but she's goin' home to-morrow an' she generally gives me five shillings when she goes. The last day's very important."

William realised that this complicated the situation considerably. He realised, too, that as the Outlaws shared tips equally, they must share also the labours and fatigues that went to the earning of them.

"All right," he said. "We'll take him along. Perhaps"—his native optimism asserted itself—"he won't be so bad, after all."

"He will," said Ginger gloomily. "You don't know what he's like. He's called Sweetikins."

This information successfully damped even William's

optimism, and it was a gloomy trio that went round to Ginger's house after lunch to call for Ginger and Sweetikins.

"I've seen it," said Douglas. "It's so fat it can hardly see, an' it can't walk at all. It jus' eats all day an' when it's not eatin' it's snappin' at people."

"I've seen it too," said Henry. "You can hear it breathin' a mile off, an' when it does walk it sort of rolls along an' sits down every step to snort."

"Oh, well," said William philosophically, "you can't expect five shillin's for nothin'."

Ginger's aunt was a stout, handsome woman, who bore a faint but unmistakable likeness to her pet. Like Sweetikins, she waddled when she walked, and breathed audibly as if always slightly out of breath.

She appeared on the doorstep holding Sweetikins in her arms. Sweetikins, a corpulent Pom, with one white ear and a white star on his forehead, was snorting like a small, dyspeptic war-horse. Ginger stood gloomily in the background.

"Now, children," said his aunt, "I want you to be very, very careful with him. He's had quite a light lunch of boiled chicken and gravy, as I didn't want him to take exercise after a heavy meal. He gets tired *very* quickly, and you must *always* let him sit down and rest when he's tired. You must *never*, of course, pull him along by his collar. In fact, I've fixed his collar so that you can't. He's got a beautiful nature, but he can't be driven. He must be led. Now, boys, I hope that you realise that it's a great honour for you to be allowed to take out my little pet. I hope that you'll show your appreciation of it by doing all you possibly can for his happiness and comfort." She espied Jumble suddenly at the back of the group. "And please don't let that great rough mongrel go near him."

But, even as she said this, Jumble gave one look of

"NOW, BOYS," SAID GINGER'S AUNT, "I HOPE YOU REALISE THAT IT'S A GREAT HONOUR TO BE ALLOWED TO TAKE OUT MY LITTLE PET."

disgust at Sweetikins and walked disdainfully away, not to be seen again till the evening. Ginger's aunt seemed relieved by his disappearance.

"Now, don't hurry my darling, whatever you do. It upsets his nerves. And, of course, don't let him out of your sight for a second. But I'm sure you wouldn't do that. Good-bye, my little precious. Bring him home in good time, boys. Bye-bye."

She gave the lead to Ginger and stood at the front door watching them till they were out of sight. It was a slow and dejected procession, suggesting, indeed, mourners behind an invisible hearse rather than boys out with a dog. Sweetikins, though he moved quite briskly from side to side as he walked, covered very little actual ground. As soon as they reached the road he sat down, panting noisily, and showed every sign of settling down to his afternoon siesta on the spot. In vain did they urge him and even propel him forward. He snarled and snapped and, immediately pressure was relaxed, sank once more into somnolence. They understood what Ginger's aunt had meant by saying that she had fixed his collar so that they could not pull him along by it. It was fastened so loosely that when they tried to pull him by it against his will his head slipped through the aperture. It was impossible, too, to tighten it. Sweetikins's mistress had seen to that. Finally William pocketed the collar and lead as useless, and Ginger picked up Sweetikins and carried him over a stile and across several fields. He was remarkably heavy for his size, and Ginger was glad at last to hand him over to William. He registered his annoyance at being thus disturbed by biting William's ear and scratching his neck. William handed him to Henry. He scratched Henry's face and chewed a button off his coat. Henry offered him to Douglas. Douglas declined him. He curled up on the grass at their feet and began to snore.

"Well," said William bitterly. "A nice afternoon we're going to have!"

"Let's try him this way," said Ginger, propelling him gently and firmly along the ground with his foot.

Sweetikins, still curled up as for sleep, bit savagely at

Ginger's ankle. They all joined in the fray and retired, worsted.

"He's bit right through my stocking," said Henry.

"You said we might find wild beasts," said Douglas sarcastically. "Well, we've found one all right."

William was gazing round the landscape.

"Tell you what," he said excitedly. "Let's push him in the old quarry."

The old quarry lay at the farther end of the field where they were. It was very deep, and its sides shelved away inwards from the top except at one point where the side went sheer down from top to bottom. The Outlaws used to descend at this point by the simple process of sliding down in a sitting position—a process that accounted for many casualties in the seats of their knickers. They generally left the quarry by way of a tree that grew conveniently from the bottom of the quarry and just reached the level of the field. The spot was one of their favourite haunts.

"Do you see?" went on William eagerly. "We'll take him down there an' he can't possibly get out 'cause he can hardly walk, much less climb, an' he'll have a nice sleep, an' we can have a good afternoon explorin', an' then we'll call for him on the way back, an' she'll never know he's not been out with us all the time. Look!" He saw some sacks on the edge of the next field and caught one up with a whoop of triumph. "Look! He can sleep on this an' he'll enjoy himself far more than if he'd been walkin' with us."

"An' so will we," said Ginger feelingly.

"Come on. I'll take him down," said William.

He bundled Sweetikins under one arm, the sack under the other, and, placing himself upon the impromptu "chute", made his way to the bottom of the quarry. Sweetikins, annoyed by this sudden and unexpected descent, uttered a shrill, indignant bark and bit William's chin.

They reached the bottom in comparative safety, and William at once set about providing a comfortable shelter for his pet. He found one under a piece of overhanging rock, where even if it rained Sweetikins's precious person would not be damped, carefully arranged the sack, and put Sweetikins upon it. Sweetikins, though he felt obliged to express his independence by snarling and snapping at William's ankles, evidently quite approved of the arrangement. He settled down upon the sack with a snort of content and passed at once into a heavy doze. William returned to the upper air by way of the tree and rejoined his companions.

"Gosh!" said Ginger, expressing the general sentiment. "Isn't it fine we've got rid of him! I feel as if I'd been dragging him about for months an' months."

Douglas felt some qualms of conscience, but he soon quieted them.

"After all," he said, "it's what Joseph's brethren did to him, an' a thing can't be wrong if it's in the Bible."

Freed of the restraint of Sweetikins's presence, the Outlaws leapt exuberantly to the wood, jostling each other and racing each other in sheer lightness of heart.

They had quite an enjoyable afternoon. It did not, perhaps, yield them all they had hoped for in the way of discoveries. They found no wild beasts or hitherto unexplored territory. But they made a fire and dammed a stream and climbed trees and were chased by a keeper, and altogether had two crowded hours of glorious life instead of the age without a name that Sweetikins's company had promised them.

Stimulated and uplifted by adventure, they returned

to the old quarry to collect their companion. And there they encountered their first reverse. They stood around the edge and gazed down in silence.

"He mus' be there," said William at last. "He *mus'* be."

"'Course he mus'," affirmed Ginger. "It's jus' the light that makes it look as if he wasn't. He's in the shadow, you see. . . . I'll go down an' get him."

He slid down to the bottom of the quarry and went to the overhanging rock where the sack could be plainly seen. He took out the sack and shook it carefully as if Sweetikins might be concealed in one of the folds. Then he began to hunt about the crevices near the overhanging rock, calling: "Hi, boy!" and even bringing himself to utter the objectionable name "Sweetikins!" But no Sweetikins appeared. He began to hunt round the quarry, still calling: "Hi, boy! Sweetikins. Come on then! Rats! Rabbits!" then, remembering Sweetikins's tastes and character, changing his appeal to: "Hi, boy! Boiled chicken and gravy!"

But still no Sweetikins appeared, and the anxiety of the watchers above increased.

"Come on. Let's all go down," said William.

They tobogganed down the chute, landing in a heap together at the bottom.

"He's not here," Ginger greeted them gloomily as they sorted themselves out.

They searched every corner of the old quarry. They called: "Hi, boy! Sweetikins! Boiled chicken!" in every tone of threat, command, entreaty, but all in vain. No Sweetikins appeared.

"Even if he'd died, we'd have found his dead body." said Ginger.

"He *can't* have climbed out," said William.

"P'raps he's been eaten by rabbits," suggested

Douglas. "He wouldn't fight a mouse, much less a rabbit."

"Well, even then," objected Henry, we'd have found bits of his fur about."

"Gosh!" said Ginger faintly. "Won't my aunt be *mad*!"

"We'll all come with you to her," said William.

"That won't make it any better," said Ginger, and added in a faint voice, overpowered by the sheer horror of the situation: "Gosh, she'll carry on something *awful*!"

"P'raps we'll find it on the way home," said Henry, but without much hope.

. They climbed back up the tree and went home very slowly, searching every inch of the ditches and hedges as they went. But neither ditch nor hedge, nor any of the neighbouring fields that they included in their search, yielded the stout, wheezing figure of Sweetikins.

"Perhaps he's gone home," suggested Douglas.

"There's going to be an awful row if he has," said Ginger despondently.

"Well, there's going to be a still bigger one if he hasn't," William reminded him.

They reached Ginger's house, surreptitiously searched the garden, then retreated to Ginger's bedroom by way of the back stairs with a vague idea of barricading themselves there against fate.

"I say," said William in a conspiratorial whisper, "we never looked in the greenhouse or the coal-shed. S'pose he's there?"

"How could he be?" said Ginger.

"Well, he might be. You never know. Anyway, I'll jus' go down an' look."

"S'pose you meet her?"

"Oh, I'll make up some yarn."

"Yes, an' get us into a worse row than we're goin' to get into."

"We couldn't get into a worse row than we're goin' to get into," said William simply.

He crept down the back stairs and into the hall and into the garden and there, as he was making his way round to the summer-house, ran full tilt into Ginger's aunt, issuing from the front door dressed in her outdoor things.

"Oh, there you are!" she said irritably. "How late you are! I thought you'd be back hours ago. Have you taken Sweetikins indoors? Now listen. I want you four boys to come with me to the Vicarage. The Vicar's wife's holding a meeting there of her Kindness to Animals League, and someone forgot to send the notices out, so she's been round this afternoon, and I've promised to go and promised that you four boys shall go. We're late already, and we'll have to hurry. I shall be on the platform, of course, so you boys must behave very nicely. Now go in quickly and take Sweetikins up to my bedroom—I've put his basket just by the fire and he'll find his tea all ready, a nice little bit of freshly cooked chicken breast, because I'm sure he'll be hungry after his long walk—and then get the others and come along *quickly* to the Vicarage. I shall expect you to have caught me up before I reach it."

And she waddled off down the road with a gait strongly reminiscent of Sweetikins's own.

Ginger ran upstairs to tell the Outlaws of this latest development of the situation.

The Kindness to Animals League was one of the Vicar's wife's pet cranks, and the Outlaws had, of course, been enrolled as unwilling members of it. Every month she held a meeting and gave a medal for the most deserving act of kindness to an animal. As no notices hàd been received this month, the Outlaws had hoped that they were going to escape a meeting. They knew that Bertie Franks, one of their greatest enemies, was

THE OUTLAWS, BUSY WITH THEIR OWN PROBLEM, TOOK LITTLE HEED. SUDDENLY, HOWEVER, THE VICAR'S WIFE WAS LEADING THE SMILING BERTIE TO THE EDGE OF THE PLATFORM.

anxious to win a medal. He had, in fact, boasted that he would win the next one.

"I thought we were goin' to miss that rotten show," grumbled Ginger.

"Well, it puts the row off a bit, anyway!" said William.

"AND NOW, DEAR CHILDREN," SHE WAS SAYING, "I WANT
YOU ALL TO GIVE DEAR BERTIE A CLAP FOR WINNING THIS
MONTH'S MEDAL."

"Yes, but only about an hour," said Ginger gloomily,
"an' it's got to come in the end."

"Oh, do shut up grumblin'," said William. "Anything might happen before then. The end of the world
might come."

"No, it won't," said Ginger with determined gloom.
"I never have any luck."

"Well, hurry up, anyway," said Henry, "or she'll be

coming up for us an' then there'll be a row all right."

At this reminder, the four of them hurled themselves down the stairs, smoothing their disordered hair and straightening their crumpled collars and pulling up their rucked stockings as they went.

They overtook Ginger's aunt at the door of the Vicarage. She looked at them with grim disapproval.

"How shockingly dirty and untidy you look, boys!" she said. "I only hope that you haven't got my Sweetikins as dirty and untidy as you've got yourselves."

They entered the parish room, where Ginger's aunt ushered them into four seats in the front row, then herself mounted the platform.

Already the Vicar's wife was on the platform together with Bertie Franks, who wore a smug expression, and a large medal pinned upon the lapel of his Eton suit. One of his hands was ostentatiously bandaged.

The proceedings began, but the Outlaws, busied with their own problem, took little heed of them. Suddenly, however, they were jolted ruthlessly out of their dreams. The Vicar's wife was leading the smiling Bertie by the hand to the edge of the platform.

"And now, dear children," she was saying, "I want you all to give dear Bertie a clap for winning this month's medal for kindness to animals." A faint-hearted round of applause greeted this announcement. "And I want you all to listen very carefully while I tell you what dear Bertie has done. You know, dear children, that some wicked people try to get rid of their dogs in order not to have to pay the licence. The deed of kindness that dear Bertie has performed is to rescue one of these poor dogs whose cruel owner tried to get rid of it in this way. Dear Bertie found this poor doggie abandoned in the old quarry. Now just try to imagine the feelings of the poor doggie left there by its cruel owner to die. But dear Bertie saw it and, at very great personal danger, dear Bertie went down to rescue it. I've only just heard about it myself because dear Bertie has only just told me about it. He's put the dear doggie in the summer-house, so that we can all go and look at it afterwards. I've not even seen it myself yet, because, through this unfortunate mistake about the notices, I've had to be rushing round ever since lunch and simply haven't had a second even to peep in at the summer-house where the dear doggie is. But Bertie has described him to me so that I can tell you all about him, just as if I'd seen him myself. He's a darling Pom, with one white ear" (Ginger's aunt sat up very straight and blinked), "and a white star on his forehead." Ginger's aunt rolled a terrible eye in the direction of the Outlaws.

"I don't know how long the dear doggie had been there, but I'm afraid a long time, because dear Bertie says that it is terribly, *terribly* fat, and perhaps you know, dear children, that one of the effects of starvation is to cause the body to swell. And he won't eat even a dog biscuit, Bertie says, which shows that he must have starved so long that his poor little appetite has quite gone. In fact, I'm afraid that he must have suffered dreadfully, because he's in a terribly nervous and irritable state and bit poor Bertie several times on the way. So that I think you'll all agree with me that dear Bertie deserves a medal for bravery as well as kindness to animals, but we mustn't blame the poor doggie who'd been left in that terrible place for days or perhaps weeks. Left to starve by his cruel owner! Now, as soon as I've finished speaking, dear children, I want you all to go out to the summer-house in the garden, because I've got the dear doggie there for you all to see, and if any of you know whose doggie it is I want you to tell me and I'll report the matter at once to the Society for the Prevention of Cruelty to Animals—a dear little brown Pom doggie with a white star on its forehead and one white ear.''

Ginger's aunt was growing redder and redder, while the eye she turned upon the Outlaws would have made a strong man quail. William began to cough so uncontrollably that the tears ran down his cheeks, and, still choking, he rose and hurried from the room, obviously in order to ease his paroxysm by fresh air or a draught of water. It was a trick that he had acquired and brought to perfection just lately for dealing with the many crises that arise in school life, but his over-frequent use of it had aroused suspicion and it was now useless as far as school was concerned, though still fairly useful outside school.

Ginger gazed after him rather bitterly. Of course it was his row, not William's, and William had every right to get out of it as best he could. But still . . .

The Vicar's wife continued to dilate on the presumed sufferings of the abandoned dog. When she had said everything that possibly could be said on the subject several times over, she gave the order for her audience to follow her into the garden.

"Come very quickly, children. I want you all to look at the dear doggie through the summer-house window, and if any of you know the cruel owner you must speak up at once. . . . "

They surged towards the door. Ginger had wild thoughts of flight, but his aunt, who looked now on the verge of apoplexy, laid a firm hand upon his collar and said grimly: "You come with me."

They swarmed out of the door and across the lawn. They swarmed round the summer-house, pressing their noses against the windows. And there on a table in the middle of the summer-house stood a large, fluffy toy dog. Quite obviously a toy dog. Such a toy dog as one would think could never be mistaken for a real one.

"It's Baby's," shouted Henry excitedly.

Henry's small sister had just arrived in her pram with her nurse in order to escort Henry home for tea. She promptly corroborated Henry's words, stretching out her arms and crying: "Baby's . . . Baby's . . . "

Then she proceeded to scream with fury until someone rescued the toy dog from the summer-house and put it into her arms. The Vicar's wife turned to the pale and stammering Bertie.

"Really, Bertie," she said irritably, "you ought to know better than that. You've merely brought up a toy dog that someone had dropped over the edge of the quarry. You must be *very* short-sighted. And no wonder it wouldn't eat dog biscuits! I'm surprised at you. You've made yourself and me ridiculous over the affair."

"B-b-b-but it was a real dog," gasped the bewildered Bertie. "Look!" He held out his bandaged hand. "Here's where it bit me."

"Nonsense!" snapped the Vicar's wife. "You must have caught your hand on some wire protruding from the paws or tail or something. I never heard of anything so absurd! Now, don't argue, Bertie, I don't want to hear another word about it. You're a very foolish boy, and I hope you'll never do such a silly thing again. Thinking it was a real dog! I never heard of such nonsense. Give me the medal back." She unpinned the medal from his coat.

"Please go home now, children. I feel very much upset by Bertie's foolish mistake."

"But it was a real dog," wailed poor Bertie again.

"Do stop making excuses, Bertie," snapped the

Vicar's wife. "It's extremely silly of you. And tell your mother to take you to an oculist as soon as possible. There must be something seriously wrong with your eyesight. Even I would never think that that was a real dog, and I'm notoriously short-sighted. Now please go home at once, because I've got quite a headache with all this upset. And *please* be more careful another time."

Still muttering: "But it *was* a real dog," the bewildered Bertie set off homeward.

Ginger looked round the group. In the forefront was Henry's sister in her pram, burbling excitedly over her recovered toy, while her nurse expatiated on the mystery to those around her. "Well, I can't think how it got to be at the bottom of the quarry. It must have been there, of course, if that's where it was found, but she had it in the garden only this morning. It'll be one of Master Henry's tricks, I'll be bound."

Ginger saw at once what must have happened. William had slipped from the room under cover of his famous coughing trick, and had rescued Sweetikins from the summer-house. Then, slipping across to Henry's house that was just opposite the Vicarage, he had snatched the toy from the garden or from Henry's sister's pram, had put it in the summer-house in place of Sweetikins, and then hurried back with Sweetikins to Ginger's house.

Ginger's aunt had loosened her hold on Ginger's collar. She was blinking in a bewildered fashion and gazing at the toy dog that Henry's sister was now flinging out of her pram in order that it might be picked up by the long-suffering nurse. It was a game of which Henry's sister never tired.

"Come along home, dear," said Ginger's aunt rather faintly. "It's all been very foolish and quite a waste of time. Are you ready, dear?"

There was a strange and unusual meekness in Ginger's aunt's manner. He accompanied her home, and there met William coming out of the side door. William looked flushed and breathless; Sweetikins was not a restful fellow-traveller.

"Well, William," said Ginger's aunt, still in her strangely chastened mood, "come up with us and see how my little Sweetikins is after his walk."

They accompanied her upstairs to her bedroom. There upon the hearthrug sat Sweetikins, now wearing his collar and guzzling boiled chicken. Ginger's aunt gazed upon him fondly.

"The darling!" she said. "Oh, the darling! He was so tired by his long walk, I expect, that he's had a nice little sleep and now he's awake and is having his tea, bless him! Well, duckums, did 'ums have a nice walkums, den?"

Sweetikins looked up and snarled eloquently. He was telling her, of course, all about his ignominious descent into the quarry, his still more ignominious rescue, his imprisonment in the Vicarage summer-house and his journey home with that objectionable boy. William had often wished that human beings could understand the language of animals, but now suddenly he felt glad that they could not.

"And now, boys," said Ginger's aunt, turning to them, "I'm afraid that I've been wronging you very deeply in my thoughts. I won't tell you what I suspected you of, because I'm sure you'd hardly believe me if I did, but I'm afraid that it was something very bad indeed, and I feel very much ashamed of having harboured such an unjust suspicion. So, to make up for it, dear boys, I'm going to give my nephew ten shillings instead of the five I usually give him. I'm afraid that when I was wronging him so in my thoughts a few minutes ago I had decided not even to give him that. But here is the ten shillings, dear boy."

Ginger took the ten-shilling note, thanked her courteously, and walked sedately out of the room with William. They walked sedately down the road, to where Henry and Douglas awaited them.

"Look here," said Henry, "where did the kid's dog come from, and where's the real dog and—what's jolly well happened?"

Ginger waved the ten-shilling note in their faces.

"*This* has happened," he said.

The four Outlaws turned cartwheels in the middle of the road.

"Three cheers for Sweetikins!" they shouted.

## Chapter 3

# William and the Real Laurence

William was walking jauntily along the road from Hadley. The usual Christmas fair was visiting the town, and William had spent a very enjoyable afternoon riding upon merry-go-rounds, flying in flying-boats, sliding down helter-skelters, tossing on Wild Sea Waves, eating a cheap and nauseous toffee mixture that pulled out like elastic, and making violent if ineffective attempts to hit coco-nuts and Aunt Sallies. He was dishevelled and penniless but blissfully happy. He was still conscious of a delicious internal sensation that was the result of the mingled motions of the merry-go-rounds, flying-boats, helter-skelter, and Wild Sea Waves. He had an untouched packet of the elastic toffee in his pocket. He carried a coco-nut that had been given to him by a man who had knocked it off its stand first shot. He was, in fact, as perfectly happy as a boy can be. He was just indulging in a pleasant day-dream, in which an enlightened parliament had decreed that every boy must attend a fair instead of school, when he almost ran into another boy who stood at the end of the road gazing wistfully in the direction of the fair-ground.

"I say," he said, "is that a fair down there?"

"Yip," answered William through a mouthful of elastic toffee.

"You just been to it?"

"Yip."

"How long is it going on?"

"To-day's the last day."

The boy looked at William very thoughtfully. Slowly something of his wistfulness vanished and the light of a great purpose began to shine in his eye.

"Where are you going?" was his next question.

"Home to tea," answered William.

"What are you going to have for tea?"

Somehow William did not resent this catechism. The light of the great purpose in the boy's eye had aroused his curiosity and communicated a vague feeling of excitement to him.

"Jus' bread and jam," he said, "an' a bit of cake if I'm lucky."

"Would you like a jolly good tea—lots of iced cakes and chocolate biscuits and jelly an' nice things like that?"

"You bet," said William.

"Well, look here." The boy threw a conspiratorial glance around and sank his voice almost to a whisper. "Would you like me to tell you how to get it?"

"You bet," said William again.

"Well, you see, it's like this," began the boy slowly. "I've come over here by train from Allington to have tea with my godmother, who's come to live in Hadley. Well, I jolly well want to go to this fair. I'd always rather go to a fair than do anything else. You've been to the fair, and you're only going home to tea, so if you'll go to my godmother's to tea instead of me I can go to this fair and have a jolly nice time."

"But she'll know I'm not you," objected William.

"No, she won't. She's never seen me since I was a baby. She's been out of England for years. Go on," he added persuasively, "be a sport. She'll give you a jolly fine tea."

"How do you know she will?" countered William. "She might only give me bread and jam and a mingy bit of cake same as I get at home."

"No, she won't. My mother says she always used to give jolly good teas when she had children to tea. Jelly and trifle and chocolate biscuits and iced cakes," he repeated, lingering temptingly over the words.

William's mouth had watered at the mention of those dainties, but, greatly as he desired them, he could not blind himself to the difficulties of the situation.

"But, look here," he said, "she'll ask me about your family an' things like that an' I'll say the wrong things an' she'll find out an' be mad."

"No, that'll be all right," the boy assured him earnestly. "Honest, that'll be all right. I've got a letter for her from my mother telling her all the family news she can possibly want to know, so she won't need to ask you anything."

William considered the situation in silence. It sounded simple enough, but he had learnt from experience to distrust situations that sounded simple.

The lilting if strident notes of mechanical music seemed to grow louder and more enticing. The boy gazed longingly down the road in their direction.

"Be a sport," he pleaded again urgently. "I'll get into an awful row if I don't go, but you're just about my size and my age, an' if you go she'll never know it's not me. You see, she's only come over to England for a visit an' she'll only have time to meet people about once, so prob'ly she'll never see me again. Anyway, if she does it'll be me that'll get into the row then, an' I'll chance it. Go on. Be a sport," he admonished again. "She might give you a tip. You can keep it if she does. I got a lot of

money at Christmas. Go on. I'll do the same for you if
ever you want me to."

"I'm not likely to want you to," said William. "My
godmother knows what I look like an' gives rotten teas
anyway."

But he was weakening, influenced less by the thought
of the tea and the tip than by the strong spice of
adventure that the situation contained.

"All right," he said at last. "Tell me where she lives
an' I'll do it."

The boy gave a whoop of joy, took a letter from his
pocket, thrust it at William, and set off at a run down the
road towards the fair.

"Hi!" shouted William. "I don't know your name."

Faintly the breeze brought back a name that sounded
like "Laurence Redwood", but already the boy was out
of sight speeding to the fair like an arrow to its mark.

William stood still, gazing at the letter in his hand,
overwhelmed suddenly by the magnitude of the adventure he had embarked upon.

"Hi!" he shouted again and began to run down the
road in the direction of the fair-ground, intending to tell
the boy that he had changed his mind, but the boy had
already entered the fair-ground and was swallowed up
by the seething mass of merry-makers, and was in fact at
that moment in the process of taking his seat in a
flying-boat.

Slowly William turned to walk back towards Hadley,
examining the letter as he did so. It was addressed to
Mrs. Maddox, Mount Cottage, East Road, Hadley.
There was something vaguely ill-omened about the
name Maddox, and William felt an impulse to tear up
the letter and go home to his tea as if he had never met
the boy. But he realised that he had definitely undertaken the project and could not now in every decency

abandon it. Moreover, if the boy's accounts of his godmother's hospitality were correct the situation would have its redeeming features.

He drew up his stockings, cleaned his shoes on the grass by the roadside, wiped his face with a grimy handkerchief, stroked back his hair with his hands, hid the coco-nut in the ditch where he could find it again, and, rendered thus a comparatively respectable object, made his way slowly to East Road.

Mount Cottage stood at the corner of the street—a snug, square little house with a green door and white lace curtains. William stood for a few moments at the gate, summoning up his courage, and then, drawing a deep breath, walked up to the front door and rang the bell. The door was opened by a woman who was evidently Mrs. Maddox herself. She belied her ominous name, looking mild and pleasant and motherly.

"It's Laurence, isn't it?" she greeted him, with a beaming smile. "Come in, dear. Nice to see you after all these years."

William entered, experiencing a swift sinking of the heart as the door closed behind him. Too late now to extricate himself from the situation, whatever might come of it. Mrs. Maddox, however, was still smiling at him benignly with her head on one side.

"I saw you last when you were about two months old, love. And I do believe I can still see the likeness. I believe I'd have almost recognised you again, wouldn't you, Charles?"

Evidently there was a Mr. Maddox. A small, white-haired man had joined her in the hall and was also surveying William with smiling interest. He, too, looked mild and amicable.

"It's Laurence, dear," said Mrs. Maddox. "My godson, you know. We saw him when he was a baby. I

was just saying I'd have recognised him again though
he's grown such a big boy."

"How d'you do, my boy?" said Mr. Maddox genially.
"Very nice to see you. Have you come by train?"

"No," said William and hastily corrected it to:
"Yes."

"And he's brought a nice long letter from his
mother," went on Mrs. Maddox, "so let's go and sit
down in the drawing-room and read it. I'm sure
Laurence is tired with his journey."

William accompanied them into the drawing-room
and fixed a stony stare on them while they read the
letter, steeling himself to parry as best he could any
questions they might ask him. But such questions as they
did ask him were quite harmless.

"So little Lucy's better?" said Mrs. Maddox.

"Oh, yes," agreed William. "She's better all right."

"And how nice that little Jack's doing so well at
school."

"Yes," agreed William. "That's jolly nice. Yes,
we're jolly glad about that."

"What a pity about Nunky's accident!"

"Yes," agreed William vaguely. "Yes, that was a pity
all right."

"I'm sure you all miss him very much."

"Oh, yes," said William, wishing that he'd asked the
real Laurence a little more about his family affairs.
"Yes, we miss him. We all miss him a lot."

"But he was very old, wasn't he?"

"Oh, yes," said William, and was going to add
"about ninety," when Mrs. Maddox went on: "Over
thirteen years old, your mother says, and, of course,
these old dogs can't get out of the way of the traffic very
well."

"No," said William, relieved that he had not committed himself on the subject of Nunky's age, who was evidently a dog and not a favourite family uncle as he had at first supposed. "No, they jolly well can't."

"I'm sorry your mother's been poorly. How did she seem to-day when you left her?"

William considered for a moment, then replied guardedly:

"Well, in some ways she seemed better, and in others she seemed worse."

He was afraid that this might seem almost too noncommittal, but evidently it didn't. Mrs. Maddox merely sighed and said: "Yes, it's so often a case of up and down." ·

"Your father all right?" said Mr. Maddox.

"William decided to retain the non-committal note that was being so successful.

"In a way he is," he answered, "and in another way he isn't. He's up and down too."

"Of course," said Mrs. Maddox with a sigh. "We none of us get any younger. And what's the new baby to be called?" she went on.

William was vainly searching in his mind for some non-committal name when Mr. Maddox broke in.

"Well, I'm sure Laurence doesn't want to sit here all afternoon telling us about his family," he said heartily. "Come in and have some tea, my boy."

William rose with alacrity to follow his host and hostess across the hall to the dining-room. And there was spread a feast to which even Laurence's description had failed to do justice. There was fruit salad and blancmange as well as jelly, and doughnuts as well as iced cake and chocolate biscuits.

"You see, I haven't forgotten what boys like," smiled Mrs. Maddox. "Now the more you eat the better we'll be pleased, so you can start at once."

William availed himself promptly of this permission. It was indeed a meal that seldom comes one's way. His host and hostess watched him with obvious pleasure.

"Well, I am glad to see you've got your appetite back, Laurence," said Mrs. Maddox. "In your mother's letter she says that you've had a very poor appetite since your attack of influenza, so I began to be afraid that all my trouble over this tea would be wasted."

"Oh, no," explained William as well as he could through a mouthful of doughnut. "Oh, no, my appetite's come back all right. I sort of felt it come back in the train on my way here."

"That's good," said Mrs. Maddox.

"Do you like school, Laurence?" asked Mr. Maddox.

"Yes," said William, thinking it the safest answer.

"OH, NO," EXPLAINED WILLIAM, "MY APPETITE'S COME BACK ALL RIGHT."

"What's the date of the battle of Waterloo?" said Mr. Maddox.

Now it so happened that William's persistent refusal to remember the date of the battle of Waterloo had got on the history master's nerves, and William had spent the last half-holiday of the autumn term writing it out two hundred times.

"Eighteen fifteen," he replied promptly.

"Splendid!" said Mr. Maddox, much pleased by this proof of scholarship. "Splendid! I like to see a boy profiting by the education his parents are paying for."

The whole thing was going off better than William had dared to hope. He even began to have dreams of a fairly substantial tip. After tea they returned to the drawing-room, and Mr. Maddox proceeded to show William his collection of wild flowers. William was not interested in wild flowers, but he pretended to be, asking questions that he fondly hoped were intelligent in order to spin out the process till half-past five, at which time he intended to say that his mother had told him to set off for home. Mr. Maddox, carried away on the waves of his enthusiasm, dilated on calyxes and corollas and stamens and styles and achenes to his heart's content, while Mrs. Maddox sat by the fire knitting and listening to them. Furtively William watched the clock. Only ten minutes—and then he could get up and take his leave. Never had a situation that looked so lion-like in the distance turned out so lamb-like at close quarters. William was beginning to attribute it all to his own cleverness and was already in imagination relating the adventure to his friends with shameless exaggeration when he glanced out of the window and saw a sight that froze his blood. For Miss Milton, a friend of his mother's who had known William from his babyhood, was coming up the path to the front door. William stopped in the

middle of an intelligent question, and his eyes bulged
with horror and dismay.

"I—I—I've gotter go now," he stammered. "I've
gotter train to catch. Now at once."

But he was too late. Already the housemaid was
opening the door, and Miss Milton was entering the
room.

She shook hands with her hostess, explaining that she
had a cousin who had another cousin who had a friend
who knew a friend of Mrs. Maddox's who, hearing that
Mrs. Maddox had come to Hadley, had asked her to call.
Then she threw a cold glance at William—for relations
between them were not cordial—and said:

"Well, William, I didn't expect to find you here."

William himself was past speech or even movement,
but Mr. Maddox said:

"This is Laurence Redwood, my godson. He's just
come over from Allington to have tea with me."

Miss Milton looked at William in indignant amazement. William had recovered his faculties by this time
and met her gaze with an utterly expressionless
countenance.

"But," began Miss Milton, then something of doubt
crept into the indignant amazement of her expression,
"but I could have sworn—— What did you say his name
was?"

"Laurence Redwood."

"And he's your godson?"

"Yes."

The doubt deepened. She could have sworn that it was
William Brown, but, after all, this woman must know
her own godson. And a spirited correspondence was
going on in the *Daily Torch*—the paper that Miss Milton
read every morning over her breakfast—on the subject
of "doubles", in which Miss Milton was deeply inter-

ested. Some of the letters told of most amazing likenesses. She looked at William again and the doubt vanished. She *couldn't* mistake him. She saw him every day. It *was* William Brown. He was up to some trick as usual. She turned an indignant, accusing glance on to him, but he met it unflinchingly. There was no recognition in his fixed stare. Again the doubt returned. This woman was obviously sincere and ingenuous in introducing him as her godson. And, after all, she considered again, a woman must know her own godson. It must be a case of a simply amazing likeness. To a hair they were alike. It was astounding. But no more astounding than some of the cases cited by correspondents in the *Daily Torch*. The last flicker of the doubt died away. She must write a letter herself to the *Daily Torch* describing this case. She must get photographs of the two boys and send them.

"Do you know," she burst out excitedly, "I know a boy who's the exact *image* of your godson. His name's William Brown." She turned to William. "Perhaps he's some relation of yours?"

William, who had now completely rallied his forces, shook his head.

"No," he said. "I've never heard of him."

"But it's simply *remarkable*," said Miss Milton with rising excitement. "I—I really must bring this boy to you, so that you can see the likeness. It's—almost incredible. I'll go straight back for him now. He lives quite close to my home. You really *must* see these two boys together. It's literally a phenomenon."

She shook hands with the bewildered Mr. and Mrs. Maddox, assuring them that she would be back shortly with William Brown, so that they could judge for themselves the amazing likeness between him and Laurence, and took her departure.

"I KNOW A BOY WHO'S THE EXACT IMAGE OF YOUR GODSON,"
THE VISITOR BURST OUT EXCITEDLY. "HIS NAME IS WILLIAM
BROWN."

"I've gotter go now," said William hoarsely as soon
as she had vanished. "Mother said I'd gotter go at half-
past five. Thank you very much for having me, but I've
gotter go now. Now at once."

But at that moment the telephone bell rang and Mrs.
Maddox went to answer it.

"That was your mother, dear," she said, when she

"I'VE NEVER HEARD OF HIM," SAID WILLIAM.

returned. "I'm afraid that Sybil's got scarlet fever."

"Sybil?" repeated William blankly.

"Yes. She's the sister next to you, isn't she?"

"Yes," said William with a mirthless grin. "Oh, yes."

"So I'm afraid you'll have to be in quarantine. She seemed ill this afternoon, your mother said, and they sent for the doctor, and he says that you must be in quarantine, of course. So I said that you might as well stay and spend your quarantine with us, because your mother will have her hands full with Sybil and the baby and the others. You'll be one less to look after at home anyway, won't you?"

William's eyes were glassy with horror.

"Yes," he said weakly, "yes, of course. Yes."

"So I said we'd decided to stay here while we're in England as we like this part of the world, and you can stay quietly with us till your quarantine is over. She's going to send your things round to-morrow. And you know, dear boy, I think the best thing for you to do now is to have a hot carbolic bath and go straight to bed. You can have one of my husband's night-shirts till your things come."

William stared about him wildly. He must find the real Laurence and tell him of this new development. There was no time to be lost.

"May I jus' go an' have a look at the fair first?" he pleaded.

"Of course not, dear," said Mrs. Maddox. "You're in quarantine. You must stay indoors or just go for nice quiet walks into the country for the next week or so. You don't want to go about giving people scarlet fever, do you?"

William did not answer. His mind was working quickly. Confession was out of the question. It would draw upon him the full blast of the wrath of Mr. and Mrs. Maddox, and the situation was, after all, not of his making. It was for Laurence and not for him to bear the full blast of wrath. He must somehow or other get in touch with Laurence and bring him here to deal with the crisis that he had caused.

"Well, may I go for a nice quiet walk in the country now?" he suggested.

But again Mrs. Maddox shook her head.

"No, dear, I think you'd better not. After all, you were with Sybil only this morning, weren't you? And you might be carrying hundreds of germs on you. As I said, I think that the best thing would be for you to have a hot carbolic bath and go straight to bed. You can read in bed, and I'll send a nice supper up to you. You'd like that, wouldn't you?"

"Yes," said William, with another mirthless smile.

He was picturing the real Laurence innocently returning to a home which fondly imagined him settled down to a peaceful quarantine with the Maddoxes. He was picturing his own parents searching for him with anxious fury when he failed to return from the fair in time for supper. There must be some way out of the situation if only he could think of it. He still hadn't thought of it when Mrs. Maddox came in to tell him the carbolic bath was ready. He still hadn't thought of it when he sat in bed in a strange room arrayed in one of Mr. Maddox's nightgowns, and Mrs. Maddox stood by him folding up his clothes.

"I'll take them down when I bring up your supper, dear," she said, "and give them a good baking. You'll be all right for a bit now, won't you? I've got one or two things to see to downstairs."

The prospect of being left alone in the strange bedroom with no protection against the world but Mr. Maddox's nightgown spurred William on to desperate action. As soon as he was alone he sprang out of bed, hastily put on his clothes, and, opening the window, swarmed down the drainpipe with a skill born of long practice. He crouched motionless at the bottom of it for a few minutes, hidden by a bush, and then, finding that no one had noticed his flight, crept to the hedge and through the hedge on to the road. There he stood irresolute. The idea of escaping to his own home was a

"YOU'LL BE ALL RIGHT FOR A BIT NOW, WON'T YOU?" SHE
SAID.

tempting one, but he felt a certain responsibility towards
the absent Laurence. He must find him if possible and
tell him of this latest development. He'd go to the fair-
ground and look for him. If he found him, well and good
(though perhaps neither well nor good for Laurence,
who would have to shoulder the burden of a situation
that was growing more complicated every minute). If he
couldn't find him he'd just go quietly home. He set off to
the fair-ground, running so fast that he did not see a
woman coming towards him till he had nearly knocked
her and himself down. She caught him by the arm.

"Mind where you're going, boy—why, it's William Brown."

He looked up to meet the startled gazé of Miss Milton.

"I've just been to your home for you, William," she went on excitedly, "but they said you hadn't come back from the fair yet. I want you to come with me, dear boy," she went on with rising excitement, "because I've discovered another boy who bears an almost miraculous likeness to you." Again she scrutinised him intently. "*Quite* miraculous. I've never come across anything like it. Really a phenomenon. He lives at Allington and he's visiting friends in Hadley. Come along, quickly, before he goes home."

She drew him, so dazed by this new turn of events as to be quite beyond resistance, back to the house from which he had just escaped. There she rang the bell, and, before he had time to dart back to the gate, the door was opened by Mr. Maddox himself. He stared at William in amazement.

"Here's Laurence, dear," he called over his shoulder.

"It can't be Laurence," his wife's voice replied from the drawing-room. "Laurence is in bed. I've just left him there."

"No," said Miss Milton triumphantly, "it's not Laurence. It's William Brown, that boy I told you about. Now isn't the likeness astonishing?" She turned to Mrs. Maddox, who had now come into the hall. "Literally astonishing."

As she spoke she waved her hand at William like a showman exhibiting some rare specimen. William stared in front of him with a look of desperate blankness.

"B—but it *is* Laurence," gasped Mrs. Maddox.

"No, that's just the astonishing part," said Miss Milton; "it isn't Laurence. You've told us yourself that

Laurence is in bed upstairs. Besides, I know this boy well. His mother's a friend of mine. I've known him all his life. Tell them what your name is, dear."

"William Brown," said William, still gazing in front of him with a fixed and glassy stare.

Mrs. Maddox looked from one to the other in helpless amazement. She would have taken her oath that this boy was Laurence. But, of course, he couldn't be. Why should Laurence say his name was William Brown? And this woman was obviously sincere in saying that he was her friend's child and she'd known him all her life. After all, a woman must know her own friend's child.

"It's—it's extraordinary," she said faintly. "I can hardly believe it. You—you'd swear it was Laurence. Come upstairs and look at Laurence. Come very quietly because he may be asleep by now. And don't go right into the room, because he's in quarantine for scarlet fever, and I don't want this boy to risk catching it. Come along. Very quietly, remember."

Once more William looked desperately round for escape, but already he was ascending the stairs with Mrs. Maddox in front of him and Miss Milton behind.

Very softly, her finger to her lips, Mrs. Maddox opened the bedroom door and peeped in. A look of stupefaction settled on to her features.

"He's—not there," she said.

She turned to William.

"Y-you *must* be Laurence," she cried distractedly.

"But I tell you I've known this boy all my life," persisted Miss Milton vehemently. "I know his mother and father. He lives just near me. His name's William Brown."

Suspicion was changing to certainty in Mrs. Maddox's eyes.

"Well, all I can say is he's the boy who——"

William saw that there was nothing for it but flight, immediate and ignominious. He pushed his way past Miss Milton and plunged down the stairs. The front door was mercifully open, but unmercifully a boy stood there blocking his way. William was plunging past him, too, but the boy grabbed him.

"I say, where are you off to?" he said. He no longer looked neat and clean and debonair. He looked instead hot and dusty and dishevelled as befitted a boy who had spent the afternoon gloriously at a fair. But it was indubitably the real Laurence.

Mrs. Maddox and Miss Milton had now arrived on the scene.

The boy was making profuse explanations and apologies to William.

"I'm terribly sorry to come barging in and messing everything up like this," he said, "but I've spent all my money at the fair and lost my return ticket, so I simply had to come."

Mrs. Maddox raised her hand to her head.

"Who is *this* boy?" she said in a faint voice.

"I'm Laurence Redwood," said the newcomer.

"Then who," said Mrs. Maddox, pointing to William, "is *this* boy?"

"I don't know," said the real Laurence. "He's just a boy I met in the road. You see, I wanted to go to the fair, and he wanted a good tea, and he'd been to the fair, and so, you see—well, we swopped. I mean, I let him come to you so's I could go to the fair, and it would have been all right if I hadn't spent all my money and lost my return ticket."

Little Mr. Maddox had come out of the drawing-room to listen to this recital, and in the tense silence that followed Laurence's explanation he suddenly began to chuckle. His wife joined in, and their mirth grew almost uncontrollable as the full meaning of what had happened dawned on them.

"Oh, dear," said Mrs. Maddox, wiping her eyes, "nothing does you as much good as a good laugh, does it? Well, that's the best tale I've heard for a long time. No, it wouldn't have been all right, Laurence, because Sybil's got scarlet fever, and you've got to stop here a bit till your quarantine's over."

"Oh, well, that's all right," said Laurence, who was evidently something of a philosopher. He turned to William. "How did you get on?"

Little Mr. Maddox began to chuckle again.

"He got on beautifully," he said, "And he knows the date of the battle of Waterloo. Do you?"

Laurence considered.

"More or less," he said vaguely. "I mean, I know it was either in the Civil Wars or the Wars of the Roses, but I've forgotten which."

Mr. Maddox chuckled again, as delighted by Laurence's ignorance as he had been by William's knowledge.

"Splendid! Splendid!" he said, rubbing his hands together.

"So your name really *is* William Brown?" said Mrs. Maddox to William.

"Yes."

"Well, well, well! You took us in nicely. I shall never forget it as long as I live. I shall have many a good laugh over this. Now come in all of you and have supper. There's a cold chicken, and William didn't finish all the trifle and jelly at tea-time though he did his best. I'll ring your mother and tell her, William. Will you stay to supper, Miss Milton?"

"No, thank you," said Miss Milton coldly.

She was feeling distinctly annoyed by the discovery of

the identity of William and Laurence. She had been looking forward to her first appearance in print and had got what she considered a really striking letter on the subject of the "double" already put together in her mind.

They stood at the door watching her prim, irate figure till it had disappeared from view.

Then Mr. Maddox began to chuckle again. . . .

# Chapter 4

# The Plan that Failed

The Outlaws sat round the old barn facing their perennial problem of insolvency. Ordinarily they did not worry much about it. They were accustomed to spend their pocket-money within five minutes of receiving it and to live through the next week in a philosophically penniless condition. But now it happened that Victor Jameson, who had received two footballs on his birthday, had offered one of them to the Outlaws for half a crown, the offer to remain open for a week. It was a magnificent football, obviously worth far more than half a crown, and the Outlaws had decided at once to buy it, the chief obstacle to this process being the fact that they could not muster a halfpenny, much less a half a crown, between them.

"Let's tell him we'll pay him in bits as we get our pocket-money," suggested Henry.

"I've told him that," said William, "but it's no good. He says people have done that sort of thing to him before an' he's not having any. He says that Bertie Franks will buy it next Friday for cash if we haven't got the half-crown by then."

"I asked my mother to lend me what was in the missionary box," said Douglas, "an' I said I'd pay it back out of my pocket-money, but she wouldn't even listen to me."

"There wouldn't have been more than twopence-halfpenny in it, anyway," said William. "There never is in missionary boxes."

"I thought of a jolly fine way this morning," said Ginger, "but people are so jolly mean."

"What did you think of?" said William.

"Well, they gave me sixpence for having a tooth out last month, so I told them this morning that I'd have five more out. That would just have made the half-crown, but they wouldn't let me. Just *mean*, I call it."

The clock from the village church tower struck one, and the meeting automatically dissolved itself.

"We'll all think hard at lunch an' try to find a way," said William as they walked down to the village, "an' we'll meet again this afternoon an' fix on the best one."

William, for his part, thought of several brilliant plans, but they all turned out to be impracticable. His mother, on being tactfully approached, refused with horror to allow him to pawn his Sunday suit or to hawk flowers and vegetables from door to door in the village, or to enlist as a drummer boy in the army.

"I never heard such *nonsense*, William," she said. "I can't think what makes you want to do such outrageous things."

"I want to do them 'cause I want half a crown," said William simply. "If you'll give me half a crown, I won't want to do them any more."

"Of course I won't," said Mrs. Brown firmly. "If you want half a crown you must save up your pocket-money."

"How can I save up half a crown by next Friday when I haven't got anything at all to start with?" demanded William bitterly.

But Mrs. Brown displayed the usual grown-up's complete lack of understanding.

"If you'd put a little aside each week in your money-box ready for emergencies as I'm always advising you to," she said, "you'd have your half-crown now."

William, realising the futility of arguing with such a wilfully perverted view of the situation, contented himself by a sigh indicative of patience strained to the breaking point.

"Oh, by the way," went on Mrs. Brown, "I had a letter from your Aunt Florence this morning. She asks if you'd like to go and stay a few days with her."

"Which one's that?" asked William.

William had innumerable aunts, none of whom generally displayed much desire for his company.

"I don't think you've ever met her," said Mrs. Brown. "She doesn't go away much. Would you like to stay with her for a few days, William?"

She spoke hopefully for, though she loved William as a good mother should, she appreciated the quiet and peace that reigned over the house in his absence.

"No," said William without hesitation, "I shouldn't like to go to stay with her. I don't like staying with aunts, and anyway I'm going to be very busy this week gettin' that half-crown."

Mrs. Brown sighed resignedly.

"Very well, dear," she said, abandoning the vision of peace and quietness that she had been cherishing ever since she received Aunt Florence's letter.

William set off immediately after lunch to the old barn, where he found the other Outlaws already assembled. None of them had yet evolved a plan. Douglas said that he had helped a very old man across the road, hoping that he was a millionaire and would give him a large sum of money, but it had turned out, not only that he was not a millionaire, but also that he had not wanted to cross the road. Instead of the half-crown he had presented Douglas with a box on the ear and a

"NO," SAID WILLIAM, WITHOUT HESITATION, "I DON'T LIKE STAYING WITH AUNTS."

stream of maledictions most unsuitable to his old age and venerable appearance. Henry had spent the dinner-hour in an ingenious if felonious attempt to make a false half-crown out of a toy saucepan belonging to his little sister, but the result was not encouraging.

"I don't see what good that is," said William. "It looks jus' like a squashed-up saucepan. Even a blind man wouldn't think it was a half-crown." Then, remembering the events of his own dinner-hour, added: "My mother said an aunt had written to her askin' me to go an' stay there. I said I'd jolly well got other things to do this week than goin' to stay with *aunts*."

But a great light had dawned upon Ginger's freckled countenance.

"But you mus' *go* there," he said excitedly. "She's sure to give you half a crown for a tip when you come away."

William considered this aspect of the question for the first time, but without much enthusiasm.

"Yes," he said, "me go an' have a jolly dull time an' half kill myself bein' polite an' clean an' suchlike! That's all very well for *you*. No, we'll jolly well think of another way if you don't mind."

But the end of the afternoon arrived, and they had not been able to think of another way. Reluctantly, and with the air of a martyr preparing himself for the stake, William yielded to their persuasions.

"All right," he said. "All right, I'll go an' half kill myself bein' polite an' clean an' all the rest of it. It's goin' to be a jolly easy half-crown for *you* to earn."

They praised his unselfishness, tactfully insinuating that he—and only he—could carry off such a situation.

"You'll jolly well be able to do it all right," said Ginger. "You can act polite an' clean an' all that better than anyone I know."

"Oh, yes, I'm jolly good at it," admitted William, "but it's goin' to be an awful sweat."

"Well, think of the football," said Ginger encouragingly.

"All right, I'll do it," said William, again assuming his

martyred air. "It's goin' to be *jolly* hard work, but I'll do it."

Mrs. Brown was surprised when William announced his intention of accepting Aunt Florence's invitation after all.

"Jus' till Thursday," he said. "I'll stay with her till Thursday."

"You've not been getting into trouble, have you, dear?" said Mrs. Brown, suspecting his sudden change of plans and having mental visions of impending visits from indignant farmers or neighbours.

"Of course not," said William in a voice of outraged innocence.

"I only wondered why you'd changed your mind so suddenly, dear," said Mrs. Brown, "that was all."

"Oh, just 'cause I'd like to stay with Aunt Florence," said William vaguely.

He was silent for a few minutes then assumed an exaggerated air of pathos.

"Do you want me to go away, Mother?" he said.

"Of course not, dear," said Mrs. Brown hastily.

"Because if you'll give me half a crown, I won't," he offered hopefully.

"Of *course* I won't give you a half-crown," said Mrs. Brown again with spirit.

"Oh, all right," said William, who hadn't really expected her to. "*Some* mothers," he couldn't help adding bitterly, "wouldn't rather have half a crown than their own children."

"What *are* you talking about?" said Mrs. Brown.

But William, still maintaining his air of dignified reproach, went upstairs to pack without answering her.

The next morning he set off, shiningly clean and in his best suit, to his Aunt Florence's. She met him at the station and her appearance did nothing to lessen the

fears with which he had been regarding the visit. She
was neat and prim and elderly, obviously a lover of order
and routine, but without the impaired sight and hearing
which can sometimes mitigate the rigours of such a
disposition.

"I hope you're fond of animals, dear boy," she said as
they drove from the station to her house, "because I've
got a pet who's very, *very* dear to me, and I'd like you to
be fond of him, too."

William's spirits rose. Ever an optimist, he visualised
a sporting little fox-terrier (and no existence can be
really dull when one has a terrier to share it) or at least a
parrot. A monkey was not, he thought, quite outside the
bounds of possibility. . . .

"I'm sure," went on Aunt Florence, "that you'll love
my dear pussy-cat."

His spirits dropped again. It *would* be a cat, of
course. . . .

The cab drew up at Aunt Florence's front door, and
the door opened to disclose a grim-looking maid-servant
and a large Siamese cat. Both maid-servant and cat
proved to be of peculiarly aloof dispositions. The maid-
servant, who disliked all boys on principle, ignored
William completely, and the Siamese received all his
overtures with an air of extreme hauteur, getting up and
removing itself to a distance when William attempted to
establish friendly relations with it.

"He's called Smut," said Aunt Florence fondly, "and
he's a really valuable cat. He wins *all* the first prizes
round here. Or rather"—her face clouded over—"he
did before Mrs. Hedley-Smith got her 'Smu'. I don't
care what the judges say," went on Aunt Florence
feelingly, "Smut's a better cat in every way than that
Smu, and how they can give that Smu first prize year
after year I simply can't think. Fancy a cat like Smut

getting *second* prize. It's ridiculous on the face of it. I never did like that Mrs. Hedley-Smith. . . . And the airs she put on about it! If I were a judge I simply wouldn't give that Smu a prize at all."

For the rest of the evening William had to listen to praises of Smut and depreciations of Smu and his mistress. He gathered that the two ladies lived in a state of acute animosity owing to jealousy on behalf of their pets. Aunt Florence's Smut had won all the first prizes at the local cat shows till Mrs. Hedley-Smith arrived on the scene with her Smu.

William, however, was not interested in the situation, and the long evening devoted to the discussion of it seemed to him interminable.

He was relieved at last when bedtime came. There was no doubt that so far his visit had been a success. His air of martyrdom gave him a misleading appearance of virtue, and he had managed to keep unbroken his resolution of speaking only when spoken to.

"You know, dear," said Aunt Florence before he went to bed, "I'm so glad to find that you're so quiet and well behaved. I'd been afraid you might be one of those rough, badly behaved boys one sometimes comes across."

William gave a mirthless smile and looked forward with a sinking heart to the four days—each as long as a year—that stood between him and the coveted half-crown. During the night he decided that his only hope of achieving it lay in absenting himself as much as possible from his aunt and her house. The next morning at breakfast he said:

"I think I'll go out for a nice long walk this morning, if you don't mind."

She smiled brightly.

"I'll go with you, dear boy. I, too, like a nice gentle stroll before lunch."

William gave a gasp of horror that he changed hastily into a cough.

"I'd *like* to go with you," he said politely, "but I— I've gotter go a diff'rent *sort* of walk from yours. I—I mean," he said mysteriously, "I've gotter go a *special* sort of walk. A *quick* sort of walk. Quicker than what you could go. I've *got* to."

She looked at him solicitously.

"You under doctor's orders, dear boy?" she said.

"Er—yes," said William, readily accepting the explanation. "Yes, that's what I am."

She sighed.

"Ah, well, you've got youth on your side."

"Yes," agreed William, accepting this too as an explanation. "Yes, that's what the doctor said was the matter with me. He said I'd got to walk a lot to cure it. He said I'd got to walk quicker than what or'ner'y people walked."

"Liver, I suppose?" said Aunt Florence.

"Yes, please," said William hopefully, and was disappointed when she handed him only a small piece of overdone bacon.

After breakfast he set off for his walk. On the outskirts of the town he passed a house on whose front doorstep sat an exact replica of Smut. He looked at it with interest. It must be the villain Smu, who now carried off the first prizes under Smut's dusky nose.

He soon left the little town behind him and strode on towards the open country. He walked till he found himself near a farm. There was a large, fascinating-looking barn in a field near it, and William distinctly saw a rat in the act of disappearing beneath its supports. He went nearer to investigate. Beneath the supports of the barn was a perfect warren of rat-holes. It would be a paradise for rat-hunting. William had often vaguely thought of finding a ferret and training it to hunt rats, putting it into the rat-holes one by one to bring a rat out of each. It was a fascinating idea, and he had often looked for a ferret in order to try it. He hunted for a ferret for the rest of the morning, but had to set off homeward as usual without having found one. It was as he was on his homeward way that another idea struck him, an idea so obvious that he wondered why he had never thought of it before.

Why not train a cat to go down rat-holes and catch rats just as a ferret catches rabbits? He felt that he could hardly wait a second before putting the idea to the test. The rats were there, the rat-holes were there, and— Smut was there. He hurried homeward, trying to hide his eagerness as he reached the house and to assume the expression of an invalid who has nevertheless benefited from a nice brisk walk.

"How do you feel now, my boy?" said Aunt Florence.

William assured her that his side felt much better—so much better, in fact, that he thought he'd go for another nice long walk that afternoon.

"I have to go to a meeting this afternoon," said Aunt Florence; "a lecture on Central Asia by a returned missionary. I'd thought that perhaps you'd like to accompany me."

William hastily said that he thought that wouldn't do his side any good and that what he needed was another nice long walk.

Fortunately for William's plan Aunt Florence set off for her meeting directly after lunch, leaving him in possession of the house. It was the work of a few moments to find the basket in which Smut was conveyed to and from the local cat shows, to ram him into it, and set off briskly for the open country and the rat-infested barn. No one was in sight, and William at once began his task of training Smut. Smut, however, was not in a trainable mood. Though quite accustomed to his cat basket, he was not accustomed to the cavalier fashion in which he had been crammed into it without the usual lining of soft down cushions. And he was not accustomed to being swung backward and forward as William had thoughtlessly swung the basket during his walk to the farm. He emerged bristling with outraged dignity. He was not soothed or reassured by being unceremoniously thrust head first down a rat-hole to the accompaniment of: "Go on, Smut, boy! Fetch it out!" There was no doubt at all that Smut was too large for the rat-holes, but William did not see why he should not be trained to accommodate himself to them by a little muscular compression. With this object in view he rammed the head of the unfortunate animal into several of the largest holes, cheering it on in its new task as he did so: "That's right, Smut! Jolly good, old boy! Fetch 'em out, then! Fetch 'em out!"

Smut, goaded to madness by this ignominious treatment, half suffocated, completely coated with mud, managed at last to free himself by an agile twist and fled from the scene like the proverbial greased lightning. William pursued him unavailingly for some distance calling: "Come on, Smut boy! Come on, then! Good boy! Milk, Smut, milk!"

Smut refused to listen to his cajolements, but the farm dogs came to see what it was all about, and William helplessly watched his aunt's cat streaking away over a ploughed field in the opposite direction from its home with four or five farm dogs in hot pursuit.

He went home very thoughtfully, carrying the empty cat basket, and reassuring himself as he went by stories he had heard of cats returning to their homes from far-distant places—with so much success, in fact, that on reaching his aunt's house he almost expected to find Smut's scornful, dusky face watching him through the drawing-room window. No Smut, however, was there. With a sinking heart he searched the house and garden. Smut had quite evidently not returned. The only bright spot in the situation was that William's aunt, too, had not returned. William replaced the cat basket, removed all traces of the rat-hunt from his person, and went again. He hung about the neighbourhood till he saw his aunt come in, gave her a few minutes to discover her loss, then entered the house with an elaborately innocent air, as if he had just come in from his walk. He found his distraught relative ransacking the house from top to bottom.

"He's gone, William," she said. "My Smut . . . he's gone. . . . Oh, what *shall* I do?"

William acted his part of surprise, dismay, and sympathy very well. If anything he rather overacted it, but his aunt was in no state to notice subtle shades of manner.

He joined in the search for some time, then, feeling that his facial muscles needed a respite from the intensity of their expression of anguish and surprise, suggested going to continue the search alone outside.

"Yes, dear boy, do," gasped Aunt Florence. "I simply can't understand it. He's never even tried to go out alone before."

William, actuated by a sincere desire of finding the missing cat, carried out a thorough examination of the neighbouring streets and gardens, but without success. He returned to find Aunt Florence placing saucers of milk at the front door, the back door, the side door, on all the window-sills, with a vague idea of luring home her errant pet.

William renewed his expression of sympathy and concern. Aunt Florence accepted his sympathy with gratitude, telling him long stories of Smut's almost superhuman intelligence, and working herself up into a state of hysterical grief at his disappearance.

"If he's not back in time for the show next week, I don't know what I shall do. I shouldn't be a bit surprised," she added darkly, "if that Mrs. Hedley-Smith isn't at the bottom of it. I've always known she was an unscrupulous woman. She knows that my Smut ought to have the first prize and she's afraid of his getting it." William continued his ministrations of condolence, but as the evening grew on he noticed that she became rather thoughtful. Once she said: "What time did you go out, William?" and more than once he saw that she was looking at his hands, which were covered in scratches as the result of his brief rat-hunt with Smut. He hastened to explain the scratches—perhaps with unnecessary vehemence and at unnecessary length—saying that he had tripped over a stone on the road and fallen into the hedge during his walk. She received this explanation without comment, merely saying after a pause:

"Has Mrs. Hedley-Smith ever spoken to you, William?"

He could see that she was beginning to harbour vague suspicions against him, connecting him in some way with the disappearance of Smut and even wondering if he had been suborned by the villainous Mrs. Hedley-Smith herself.

It was obvious the next morning that her night's meditations had not diminished her suspicions. William, on his side, had thought out a new and much more convincing explanation of his scratches, but she received it in silence. A message of condolence sent by Mrs. Hedley-Smith just before lunch seemed to increase her suspicion, and William began to realise that the half-crown for which he had undertaken this visit depended solely upon the immediate and safe return of Smut.

After lunch he said:

"Now I'm goin' out to find Smut, an' I won't come back without him."

There was no doubt that Aunt Florence was impressed by the determination of his tone and manner. She looked at him thoughtfully as if wondering whether she had misjudged him.

"I shall be *most* grateful, William, if you do," she said earnestly.

So William sallied forth, determined at all costs to secure Smut and incidentally his half-crown. He spent the afternoon searching the vicinity of the farm, but once more with no result. Coming disconsolately homeward, he passed the house of Mrs. Hedley-Smith, and there in the open gateway sat the hated Smu, washing himself complacently. He glanced up at the windows. No one could be seen. Quick as a thought he snatched up Smu, slipped him, wriggling and protesting, beneath his coat and hurried home as fast as he could.

"I've found him!" he cried as soon as he opened the front door.

Aunt Florence came running with open arms to receive her recovered pet. Smu was accustomed to be enthused over by lady admirers and suffered her attentions passively. He was a cat of phlegmatic disposition. He had been reft from his home, hustled unceremoniously along the street and carried into a strange house, but he bore no one any ill will on that account. Cream and sardines were being offered him, and he began to purr loudly. Generally speaking, one house was as good as another to Smu, but a house in which he was given cream and sardines was definitely one to be cultivated. His own mistress dieted him rather strictly, and cream and sardines were not on his regular menu.

"The darling!" said Aunt Florence. "Listen to him purring! He's so *glad* to be home again. How I wish he could tell us where he's been since yesterday. Don't you, William?"

William answered this question by a non-committal grunt.

Aunt Florence bent down to stroke the newcomer, examining it solicitously. Smut and Smu were so much alike that no one but their mistresses and the judges at the cat show claimed to be able to tell the difference between them. Their markings were indisputably identical, but Smu was a little thinner than Smut, possibly owing to the diet of cream and sardines on which the lordly Smut battened. It was, indeed, the growing plumpness of Smut that had ousted him from the position of first-prize winner.

"He's got terribly thin, poor darling,"—wailed Aunt Florence. "He can't have had anything to eat at all since he's been away. I can count his poor ribs. Oh, my darling Smutty, how you must have suffered!"

There was no doubt at all that William was completely restored to favour. Aunt Florence was almost embarrassing in her gratitude.

"I shall *never* forget what you have done for me, dear boy," she said. "I shall never forget that it was you who found my poor lost pussy-cat for me."

William, in fact, felt as if the half-crown were already in his pocket. The report that reached them later in the day that Mrs. Hedley-Smith's Smu had been lost raised Aunt Florence's spirits to a state of ecstatic exultation.

"Well, if that doesn't just serve her right," she said, "sending that nasty sneering message yesterday! I'm not surprised her cat's run away. I've always said she half starved it. First prize indeed!" Her exultation increased as a further thought struck her. "If he's not back by next week my Smut will get the first prize, won't you, my pet!" she said to Smu, who was now dozing off the effects of his cream and sardines.

It was at this point that the maid announced that Mrs. Hedley-Smith had called and had been shown into the drawing-room. Aunt Florence, her face glowing with exultation and triumph, sallied in to her. Mrs. Hedley-Smith's eyes were bright with the light of battle.

"I've come to congratulate you on the recovery of your pet," she began.

"Thank you," purred Aunt Florence. "Thank you *so* much. And I was *so* sorry to hear that your poor Smu had run away. *Such* a pity if he hasn't come back by next week!"

"I think he *will* have come back by then, Miss Brown," said Mrs. Hedley-Smith, her voice and colour rising as the lust for battle blazed yet higher in her breast. "I think, in fact, that he's not very far away from us at this moment. Will you *kindly* allow me to see the cat that you *allege* to be your Smut?"

"And what do you mean by that, Mrs. Hedley-Smith?" said Aunt Florence icily.

"What I say. I——"

But at this point Smu himself walked into the room, still purring.

"My Smu!" screamed Mrs. Hedley-Smith.

"My Smut!" contradicted Aunt Florence.

"Of *course* he's my Smu. As if I could mistake him! Why, he knows me. Smu Smu, Smu!"

"Smut, Smut, Smut!" called Aunt Florence.

Smu sat down on the carpet and looked from one to the other, still purring loudly.

William stood in the doorway, wondering what was

"OF COURSE HE'S MY SMU," SCREAMED MRS. HEDLEY-SMITH.

going to happen next. What happened next was the
advent of a boy from the farm carrying a basket. He
demanded to see Aunt Florence at once and was ushered
into the drawing-room.

"I've brought that there cat," he said.

"What cat?" said Aunt Florence faintly.

The farm boy cocked a thumb at William.

"SMUT, SMUT, SMUT!" CALLED AUNT FLORENCE. THE CAT SAT
DOWN ON THE CARPET AND LOOKED FROM ONE TO THE OTHER.

"The one he brought up rattin' to the farm. It's been
livin' in the fields round about till this arternoon an' this
arternoon I catched it."

He opened the basket, and from it there sprang a
Smut made wiry and ferocious by a return—though but a
short one—to the wild state of his ancestors. He sprang

at the usurper Smu, and in a second the prim little drawing-room was a pandemonium of fighting cats— hissing, spitting, swearing, clawing. Smu, almost completely denuded of his fur, sprang at last through the open window, closely pursued by his assailant. The two cats streaked down the road, followed by their two mistresses. It was not till a quarter of an hour later that Aunt Florence returned, hot and dishevelled, carrying a still spitting Smut under one arm. The maid-servant stood at the front door, watching dispassionately.

"And *where*," said Aunt Florence grimly, "is Master William?"

The maid-servant pointed down the road. In the distance could be seen the figure of William walking rapidly in the direction of the station, carrying his suit-case.

"'E told me to tell you," said the maid-servant, "that that thing in his side had come on bad sudden, an' he thought he'd better go home."

# Chapter 5

# Only Just in Time

William wandered dispiritedly in the direction of the old barn.

"Well?" the other Outlaws greeted him hopefully as soon as he appeared in the doorway.

He sat down morosely on a broken packing-case, his chin in his hands.

"She didn't give me a tip at all," he said.

They stared at him in dismay.

"Why didn't she?"

"'Cause she's mean," explained William simply. "She's so mean that—well, you jus' think of the meanest person you can think of an' she's meaner than that."

"Not even *sixpence*?" said Douglas.

"Not even a halfpenny," said William bitterly.

"You've come back a bit early," said Ginger. "I thought you were stayin' till to-morrow."

"Yes," admitted William. "Yes, there was a bit of a mix-up about a cat."

"Whose cat?"

"Her cat," said William. "I took it out rattin' an' it got lost an' then there was an awful fuss 'cause it was a prize cat an' wasn't s'posed to go out rattin'. Then I found it again for her, but it wasn't the right one an' then the right one I'd took rattin' came home an' had a fight with the wrong one that I'd found, an' the wrong one that I'd found's mistress came looking for it an' there was an awful mix-up an' my aunt got so mad that I came home."

The Outlaws contemplated this succinct account of William's visit to a peaceful maiden aunt in silence, then Ginger said with dispassionate interest:

"Well, then, I s'pose she'll write to your father an' you'll get into a jolly row."

"I don't think so," said William thoughtfully. "You see, this other wrong cat that I found always gets the first prize at the show an' my aunt's cat gets the second, an' after the fight this other wrong cat that I found had got all its fur pulled off an' the show's next week, so my aunt's cat'll get the first prize all right this time. No, she rang up my father an' she only said that she was sorry I'd come over ill an' gone home so sudden. You see," he explained, "I'd pretended to come over ill."

"An' what did he say?"

"He said a lot of sarcastic things an' my mother gave me a dose of castor-oil, but," he ended with quiet satisfaction, "they couldn't do anythin' more'n *that*."

"Yes, an' here we are without any money for the football," said Ginger sternly, "an' if we've not got it by eight o'clock to-morrow Bertie Franks'll get it, an' won't he jolly well crow over us!"

William's quiet satisfaction changed again to moroseness.

"I did all I could," he said with a martyred air. "I had an awful time there. She din't give me enough to eat— she only gave me one helping of meat and two of pudding—an' when she wasn't talkin' about cats she was talkin' about the League of Nations an' stuff like that."

"Well, why did you start messin' about with her cat?" said Henry accusingly.

"Oh, never mind," said Ginger, seeing that William

was about to launch into a justification of his conduct that would probably take the rest of the day. "The thing is to think of some way of gettin' that half-crown. We've not got much time."

"Well, we thought of all the ways we could think of before William went away," said Henry, "an' they weren't any good. I wish," he ended thoughtfully, "I could get some proper tools for makin' false coins. I've tried wrappin' pennies up in silver paper, but it wasn't any good."

"'Jus' stop talkin' a bit," said William, who felt that soon one or another of them would again refer to his failure to secure his aunt's tip if he did not forestall them by a timely display of severity. "You keep on talkin' an' talkin' instead of thinkin'. If you'd use your brains a bit 'stead of your tongues all the time——"

"Same as you use your brains messin' up people's cats 'stead of gettin' on with gettin' a tip," put in Douglas bitterly.

William was just gathering his breath and dignity together for a devastating retort when suddenly a little girl appeared at the open door of the barn. It was a little girl well known to the Outlaws—Violet Elizabeth Bott of the Hall. The Outlaws did not generally regard Violet Elizabeth Bott with very tender feelings. When on friendly terms with them she made herself an intolerable nuisance, and when on unfriendly terms her air of haughty scorn was unspeakably galling. She carried feminine variability and inconsistency to extremes, and, despite her youth (she was six years old), could deal effectively with almost any crisis. She had for this purpose a large armoury of offensive and defensive weapons. She could sob in a most realistically heart-broken manner at a moment's notice, and her proudest boast was that she could be sick at will. The latter gift was of great asistance to her in her dealings with her mother, who had a great regard for appearances.

She stood in the doorway, gazing at the Outlaws in silence and sucking a stick of rock. There was a limpid guilelessness in her blue eyes and in the cherubic curves

SHE STARED AT THEM OVER HER STICK OF ROCK. "WE DON'T WANT YOU," SAID WILLIAM. "GO AWAY."

of her mouth that the Outlaws had long ago learnt to distrust.

She stared at them over her stick of rock, and sucked with an air of gentle melancholy.

"We don't want you," said William brusquely. "We're busy. Go away."

Too late he remembered that this was the one way of making certain that Violet Elizabeth would not leave them till she had discovered every detail of the business on which they were engaged. Once her curiosity was aroused she was impervious to hints, snubs and even physical violence. She remained unmoved even by mockery of her lisp, for despite the cherubic perfection of Violet Elizabeth's mouth it could not pronounce the letter S.

"What are you buthy doin'?" she demanded.

"Nothin'," said William succinctly.

"You can't be buthy doin' nothin'," objected Violet Elizabeth with an air of deep wisdom. "It ithn't pothible."

"Yeth, it ith," said William, mimicking her voice and lisp in a forlorn hope of annoying her. But Violet Elizabeth took the rock out of her mouth and smiled at William with devastating sweetness.

"You are *funny*, William," she said in whole-hearted appreciation of the joke and repeated: "What are you buthy doin'?"

"Something we don't want you messing about in," said Ginger, "so you can jolly well go away."

Evidently taking this as an invitation, she entered the barn, still smiling sweetly.

"I won't meth about in it," she promised, "if you'll tell me what it ith."

They gazed at her helplessly. She handed the stick of rock to William with a gesture of friendliness.

"Have a thuck," she said generously. "Have a big thuck. Bite a pieth off if you like."

Rock was one of William's weaknesses. He bit a large piece off, trying to preserve an impassive demeanour as if he were doing it entirely without prejudice.

She handed it to Ginger.

"Bite a pieth off, Ginger."

Neither could Ginger resist the bright pink bait. He, too, bit a large piece off. Henry and Douglas, seeing the fall of their leaders, made no attempt at resistance. Each bit off a large portion, and Violet Elizabeth popped the remaining fragment into her mouth and for some moments the five of them crunched in silence. Then Violet Elizabeth, swallowing the last remnant, said once more: "What are you buthy doin'?"

Their former attitude of aloof severity seemed difficult to maintain, and William, while trying to preserve his stern tone and aspect, unbent so far as to give her the information she demanded.

"We're trying to think of a way of makin' money," he said, "so now you know and you can jolly well go away 'cause we don't want you."

"How muth money do you want?" said Violet Elizabeth, ignoring his invitation to depart.

"Half a crown."

"How muth ith half a crown?"

"Two shillings and sixpence."

"Two thillingth an' thixpenth!" repeated Violet Elizabeth, impressed. "Thath a lot of money."

"I know it is," said William. "That's why we're jolly busy thinking out a way of gettin' it, an' "—pointedly—"that's why we don't want kids knocking about bothering us."

"I won't knock about bothering you," promised Violet Elizabeth earnestly, "I'll thtay an' help you. I'll think of a way of gettin' two thillingth an' thixpenth, too."

She sat down by William, keeping so still for a few moments that it did not seem possible to object to her presence.

At last she broke the silence.

"My father knowth a man that made loth of money by night clubth."

"What are they?" demanded William suspiciously.

"They're clubth, an' people go to them at nighth an' pay loth of money."

"Well, we can't do that," said William, "so you may as well shut up about it."

"Why can't we do that, William?" she demanded earnestly. "Ith eathy enough to have a night club."

"Oh, ith it?" mocked William in a tone of withering sarcasm. "P'raps you'll kin'ly tell me where we can have it an' who'll come to it."

"Yeth, I will, William," said Violet Elizabeth, wholly unwithered by the withering sarcasm. "We can have it here an' everyone'll come to it."

"Oh, they will, will they?" said William. "Yes, they'll all likely come to a night club when they've all got to be in bed by eight, won't they?"

"We'll thut it up at eight, William. We'll have it from thix to eight. You can make *loth* of money by a night club."

"What do people do at night clubs?" said William, weakening.

"They thit at little tableth an' drink thingth," said Elizabeth. "They pay money to come in an' then they pay more money to thit at little tableth an' drink thingth."

"Well, we haven't got any little tables an' we haven't got anything for them to drink," said William finally, "an' no one would pay money to come in here, so you might as well shut up talkin' about it."

But the decisiveness of his tone did not ring quite true, and Violet Elizabeth guessed that the idea interested him despite himself.

"We needn't have tableth," she said persuasively, "not *real* tableth, William. Packing-catheth will do. They can thit on the floor round packing-catheth. An' we can get liquorith water for them to drink. I've got thome liquorith. I'll bring it to make liquorith water with. It won't cotht you anything, William, an' you'll make loth an' *loth* of money."

William hesitated and was lost.

"What else do you want for a night club?" he said.

"A cabaret," said Violet Elizabeth, whose vocabulary was in some ways more extensive than her years warranted.

William tried to hide his ignorance of the meaning of this word by adopting a haughty tone of voice.

"We've got one at home," he said. "Sev'ral, in fact. But I know my mother wouldn't let me bring one here."

"I mean thomeone to thing an' danth," said Violet Elizabeth patiently.

"Oh, that!" said William. "I don't think they'll want that."

"But they muth have it," said Violet Elizabeth firmly. "Ith a night club, an' they muth have it whether they want it or not."

"Look here," said William, stung by her tone, "don't you jolly well get too bossy. Who's running the night club—you or me?"

"You, William," said Violet Elizabeth meekly. "An' I'm not getting too bothy. I'm only tryin' to help. They *muth* have thinging an' danthing."

"Well, who'll do it?"

"I will," said Violet Elizabeth complacently. "I can thing an' danth. I'll put on a Chinese thawl of my motherth an' I'll thing and danth in it. An' then when I've finithed they can danth if they want. They do in night clubth."

"It sounds jolly dull," said William. "What else do they do in night clubs?"

"There muth be an orchethtra," said Violet Elizabeth, "an' they muth make *loth* of noith. They muth eath play thingth to make *loth* of noith."

"An' what else?" said William.

"They muth thign their namth in a book when they come in."

"Why?" said William.

"'Cause they do it in night clubth."

"Anything else?" demanded William.

Violet Elizabeth considered deeply, then brought out another choice morsel from her store of wordly knowledge.

"There muth be a raid."

"A raid?"

"A raid by the polith. Therth alwayth a raid by the polith in a night club."

William had the feeling he so often had in his dealings with this redoubtable child, a feeling of being stripped of his authority and ousted from his position as chief—and that with a sweetness and apparent pliability that gave him no handle against her.

"We'll charge them twopenth to come in," went on Violet Elizabeth, "an' twopenth for the liquorith water an' I gueth we'll make loth an' *loth* more than two thillingth an' thixpenth."

"They won't pay twopence to come in," objected William. "Not jus' to come in here. Why should they?"

"They'll pay to thee me danth an' thing," said Violet

Elizabeth complacently. "Ith worth muth more than twopenth to thee me danth an' thing."

"All right," said William, yielding to the inevitable; "we might as well try it anyway."

Secretly he was deeply interested in the idea, but wished that it had been his own and not Violet Elizabeth's.

They spent the next morning preparing the old barn and distributing handbills to the children of the neighbourhood. The handbills were drawn up by Violet Elizabeth herself and printed in red chalk on pages torn out of her copy-book.

She did not consult the Outlaws as to spelling or composition, but the result, though unorthodox, was quite clear and indeed striking.

A Nit Club
Will be hel
toonit
in the
Ole Barn
ther wil bee drinking and mee singing and darnsing
for tuppence.
*Plese Kum*

She had distributed half a dozen copies of this masterpiece before Ginger discovered it and hastily revised it. Violet Elizabeth regarded his alterations with deep suspicion.

"You're thpelling it all wrong," she said indignantly. "I took loth of trouble over it and now you're thpelling it all wrong."

Ginger, who was not without tact, told her that they wanted her help and advice in preparing the old barn. He copied out a dozen more leaflets and distributed them, making sure that each would be passed round a large juvenile circle, then returned to the old barn. Packing-cases were placed at intervals down the middle, where the patrons were to sit. Violet Elizabeth had had a sudden inspiration and had run home to purloin the "rag-bag" into which all odds and ends of material left over from dressmaking or household sewing were put. As a result each packing-case was decorated with a heterogeneous assortment of bits of lace, satin, calico, flannel, tweed, or even fur. The lighting arrangements were, of course, a problem, and here the Outlaws felt most acutely the difficulties that beset those who try to launch a night club without sufficient capital.

"They can't sit in the dark," said William firmly.

"P'raps there'll be a moon," said Ginger.

"No, there won't," said William. "It was pitch-dark last night. There couldn't be a moon sudden. They have to grow gradual."

It was finally decided that each of them should go home and there try to secure some means of lighting the premises. They returned in half an hour. Ginger had found an old bicycle lamp long since discarded by his elder brother, Henry had found a small box of Bengal Lights left over from last fifth of November, William had found a box of candle-ends that was being hoarded by the cook for some economical purpose of her own, Douglas had found an old electric torch with an exhausted battery that nevertheless showed a gleam when shaken very hard, and Violet Elizabeth had found two Chinese lanterns and a toy cooking-stove that she said would light up but that resisted all attempts to prove her statement.

A space was kept at the end of the barn for the orchestra, who were to be William and Ginger. Each were to have two instruments—William a mouth-organ and a tin tray, Ginger a trumpet and a particularly raucous rattle belonging to his elder brother that had figured in many a university-"rag". In this space, too, Violet Elizabeth was to dance and sing.

The liquorice contributed by her had turned out to be less in quantity than she had led them to expect. They had made two jugs of liquorice water with it, but it was, as William said, more water than liquorice—only a faint violet colour instead of that deep purple beloved of liquorice water connoisseurs.

"What are they goin' to drink out of?" demanded William.

"Out of the jug," said Violet Elizabeth firmly. "They can pay twopenth an' have three thwallowth eath."

It had been arranged that Douglas should hand round the drinks, while Henry took the money at the door and kept the club register.

A certain amount of excitement reigned among the youthful population of the neighbourhood. Most of those interested had only the vaguest ideas of what a night club was, but long before six a vanguard appeared in the form of a handful of children apparently under the leadership of a lanky girl, with red hair, a thin, pointed nose, and a suspicious expression.

Violet Elizabeth arrived at about ten to six, closing the door with an air of stern officialdom in the nose of the vanguard leader. She carried a parcel containing the Chinese shawl and wore an expression of suppressed excitement.

"I thay," she began, "I've arranged a thurprithe."

"What sort of surprise?" said William, who was engaged in removing the small particles of chewing gum that blocked up the hole of his mouth-organ.

"A thecret thurprithe," said Violet Elizabeth, still beaming with excitement. "I thought of it juth now. Ith a *lovely* thecret thurprithe. It'll make it an *abtholutely* real night club."

The two Chinese lanterns had been hung up in the two corners of the barn, and the candle-ends had been stuck upon the tables here and there. The bicycle lamp, electric torch, and cooking-stove had proved useless as means of illumination.

Douglas was anxiously inspecting his jugs of liquorice water. So pale had it looked that he had had recourse to the dubious expedient of colouring matter. He had on the impulse of the moment dissolved a cake of black paint from his paint box in each jug. He had assured himself that it would make no difference to the taste, and that it would save him from the vituperation of his patrons, but, now that the deed was done beyond recall, doubts assailed him. He looked uneasy and conscience-ridden. Occasionally he would dip a finger into one of the jugs and lick it with a thoughtful, far-away expression.

The church clock slowly struck six, and Henry flung open the door.

The red-haired vanguard leader, who had been leaning against it, closely applying her eye to a crack in the wood, fell forward on top of Henry, then accused him indignantly of pushing her over. Henry asked her to sign her name in the book, which was an old arithmetic exercise book of William's, scored all over, as were most of William's exercise books, in red ink. She refused. He asked her to pay the twopence entrance. She refused, but offered him instead a halfpenny which she said was enough to pay for her own entrance and that of the rest of the vanguard whom she was "minding". Henry argued and entreated. She answered him with Amazonian spirit, asking him who he thought he was anyway, and offering for two pins to "push his face in".

A large crowd was gathering behind her. Henry threw a despairing glance at the other Outlaws, but Douglas was still deeply absorbed by his liquorice water and William by his mouth-organ, while Ginger was carrying out experiments on his rattle.

Helplessly Henry let the vanguard push its way through. Other patrons then arrived. Following the vanguard's example, they refused either to sign the book or to pay more than a halfpenny. While one was paying a halfpenny two others generally squeezed in without paying anything. Last of all came Bertie Franks. He showed a half-crown ostentatiously to Henry, and he paid his halfpenny with a particularly insulting grin, a grin that said more plainly than words: "Yah! I've got my half-crown and you're a jolly long way off yours yet."

The barn was now practically full, and Henry counted his takings—twenty-four halfpennies—one shilling. They were still one and sixpence off their goal, but he looked forward hopefully to the other attractions. They might get one and sixpence for the liquorice water. Bertie was watching him count his takings, and though Henry tried to assume the jaunty air of one who has taken at least half a crown, he was well aware that he did not deceive Bertie, whose grin grew more and more exasperating every second. The vanguard leader was now making trouble about the seating accommodation and indignantly refusing to commit her precious person to the ground.

"What d'you think I've paid for?" she demanded passionately.

"Well, what d'you expect for a halfpenny?" said William, who was hastily summoned to deal with her.

"A chair," she answered simply, and continued with cold fury: "D'you think I've paid a halfpenny to sit on the ground in a draught gettin' my death? I can do that outside if I want to without payin' anything, thank you very much indeed."

So fierce she looked, her red hair and pointed nose a-quiver with indignation, that Ginger was on the point of starting off home to get a chair for her, when Henry had the brilliant idea of taking some of the "table" coverings—a corner of lace, two inches of fur, an old hot-water bottle cover and half a yard of braid—and putting them on the ground for her to sit on. Slightly mollified, but still quivering with indignation, she consented to sit on them. The other patrons followed her example and took the coverings from their tables to form seats. There was a good deal of loudly voiced depreciation of the arrangements made for their reception.

"Disgraceful, I call it," said the vanguard leader, "charging a halfpenny for sitting on the ground on old rags."

William felt that it was time for the entertainment to begin. Violet Elizabeth had put on the shawl, but she was showing herself as unreliable in a crisis as she generally did, sweeping about in its gleaming embroidery, completely engrossed in some private game of her own.

"Can't you sing or dance or something like what you said?" hissed William at her fiercely.

"Not juth now," she replied sweetly. "Juth now I'm playing I'm a princeth an' theth people are all my courtierth."

The imaginary courtiers were growing more and more restive, so William, though he had meant his orchestra to form the grand finale of the evening, decided to start it at once. He and Ginger took their seats on the floor, their instruments around them, and leapt into a riot of discord worthy of the highest tradition of jazz.

WILLIAM AND GINGER, THEIR MUSICAL INSTRUMENTS AROUND
THEM, LEAPT INTO A RIOT OF DISCORD.

Violet Elizabeth, roused by this to a sense of her
duties, began to sing. She had a shrill little voice, not
quite in tune, that rose clearly above the blare of the
orchestra. She sang "By Killarney's Lakes and Fells",
"London Bridge is Falling Down", and "Mad About
the Boy".

Douglas began to hand round the liquorice water. At
once the vanguard leader set herself to make further
trouble, refusing payment with passionate indignation.

"What have I got for that halfpenny I paid to come in?" she demanded eloquently. "That's what I want to know. If I wanted to sit on the ground and watch a set of

"WHAT HAVE I GOT FOR THE HALFPENNY I PAID?" SHE DEMANDED. "I'M NOT GOIN' TO PAY FOR A DRINK OF THAT OLE STUFF."

kids kicking up a row I could do it at home for nothing, couldn't I? I'm jolly well not goin' to pay for a drink of that ole stuff. Why, there isn't even a cup to drink it out of. What do you think we are—monkeys? . . . Here, let's taste what it's like."

She snatched the jug from Douglas's hand and took a deep draught.

"No," she informed the others, "I wouldn't pay to drink this. I'd pay not to drink it, more like. What's it made of? Ink?"

Despite Douglas's commands and entreaties, the other patrons passed the jug round, each taking experimental draughts gratis.

That was, of course, the end of the night club. The first taste of the liquid definitely suggested liquorice water, but the after-taste had a lingering unpleasantness that gradually turned to nausea. On learning that this was to be all the refreshment provided, and that the orchestra and Violet Elizabeth were to be the only entertainment, the patrons rose in a body and demanded the return of their money. In vain William argued with them.

"You don't know how to *act* in a night club," he said. "That's all they *do* in a night club. They *do* jus' sit at tables and drink an' listen to music. An' dance. You can dance if you like. No one's stoppin' you dancin' an' havin' a good time if you want to. I tell you, you don't know how to *act* in a night club."

But the vanguard leader apparently did know how to act in a night club. She made a sudden raid upon the unsuspecting Henry, plunged her hand into the pocket that contained the entrance money, and triumphantly withdrew her halfpenny.

"You're nothin more'n' robbers, that's what you're not," she said furiously as she flounced out, followed by her charges, the youngest of whom, having found the second jug of liquorice-paint unguarded, had drained it and was now loudly and tearfully proclaiming his immediate intention of being sick. The other patrons, as usual, followed the vanguard's lead—for, though only a girl, there was an impressive air of experience and decision about her. They raided Henry, took from him their entrance fees, despite all his attempts at resistance, and surged out of the barn to the accompaniment of derogatory comments on the accommodation, fare, and entertainment of the now disbanded night club. The other Outlaws had tried to come to the rescue, arguing, entreating, commanding, defending Henry and his entrance money, but the combined attack of the patrons had been too much for them. They were left, breathless, bruised, and dishevelled, amid the ruins of their night club. The last patron to depart was Bertie Franks. As he went he held up his half-crown with an irritating grin and · said:

"I'm going round for that football now. It's nearly .eight."

The Outlaws turned accusingly upon Violet Elizabeth, the originator of the scheme, but she fore-stalled them by having a *crise de nerves* on her own account.

"Why did you let them go?" she screamed angrily. "I wath juth goin' to danth. I'd made up a new danth an' I wath juth goin' to do it an' you went an' let them go. Haven't you got any *thenth*? Why did you let them go juth when I wath goin' to do my danth?"

She stopped abruptly.

A policeman had appeared in the doorway of the barn. Violet Elizabeth stamped her foot at him furiously.

"Go away," she said. "You're too *late*. Why didn't you come before? We don't want you now. They've all gone. Go *away*, I tell you."

For the policeman was the "thecret thurprithe" that Violet Elizabeth had prepared for the night club.

He was to lend the final touch of atmosphere to it. She had sent him a note: "Pleze rade ole barn between sevin an ate."

The policeman was of a credulous disposition. He was

A POLICEMAN HAD APPEARED IN THE DOORWAY. VIOLET
ELIZABETH STAMPED HER FOOT. "GO AWAY," SHE SAID.
"YOU'RE TOO LATE."

also an indefatigable reader of detective novels, and he
had just read one in which the arch criminal was a
particularly illiterate character and wrote notes spelt as
phonetically as Violet Elizabeth's. Moreover, there had
just been a sensational burglary at Lady Markham's—
less than five miles away—last night, and the police
theory was that the burglar, who had narrowly escaped
capture, had hidden the bulk of his spoils somewhere in
the neighbourhood in order to escape unhampered by

them, intending to return later. The policeman had not the faintest doubt that the note was connected with this burglary. An accomplice "squeaking", or a spurned sweetheart getting her own back. . . .

He flashed his bull's-eye lantern on the children.

"Clear out, you kids," he said shortly.

Violet Elizabeth stared at him open mouthed with indignation.

He took no notice of her, but began to make a thorough search of the old barn, moving the boxes, inspecting the walls and roof and finally turning over a pile of filthy rotten sacks that had stood in a corner ever since the Outlaws could remember.

"Whath the thenth of raiding it now," Violet Elizabeth demanded of him scornfully, "now they've all gone home? Whath the *thenth* of it?"

He began to turn over the pile of sacks one by one.

"Heth potty, thath what he ith," said Violet Elizabeth to William.

She was longing to quarrel with someone, and she was tired of quarrelling with the Outlaws. The policeman seemed a godsend. She had never had an opportunity of quarrelling with a policeman before.

"Abtholutely potty," she said again.

The policeman took no notice. He had closely examined each sack and had now got down to the bare earth beneath the pile. The earth looked as if it had been recently dug and very hastily stamped down.

He scraped it with his foot, then knelt down and began to dig with his hands.

"Abtholutely potty," said Violet Elizabeth with a note almost of wistful pleading in her voice. She *did* so want to quarrel with a policeman. . . .

But he still took no notice. He was drawing something out of the hole he had dug—another sack, newer than the others and very heavy. He opened it and peeped inside.

"Gosh!" he said faintly. "It's the stuff. . . . "

Immediately all was confusion and uproar. William was despatched to the police station. A policeman was despatched to Marleigh Manor. A young man—Lady Markham's secretary—arrived on a motor-cycle.

"But who sent the note?" he said when he had heard all about it.

"I thent the note," said Violet Elizabeth proudly. "I thent it 'cauth I wanted him to raid the club."

"I don't care why you sent it," said the young man. "It's delivered the goods all right. Now, young lady, choose what reward you'd like. If it's anything in reason I'm sure that Lady Markham will give it to you."

"I'll think about it," said Violet Elizabeth cautiously. "I won't chooth anything in a hurry. But ith *hith* club"— she pointed at William—"an' *he* wanth half a crown."

Smiling, the young man took a half-crown out of his pocket and handed it to William.

William said "Thank you," and then seemed to disappear as completely as if the earth had opened to swallow him up.

Just before eight o'clock Bertie Franks walked jauntily up the steps of Victor Jameson's house and knocked at the door.

Victor Jameson opened it himself.

"I've come for the football," said Bertie with a grin. "William's not got the half-crown."

Victor's face displayed no great enthusiasm at this news.

"You promised it me, you know," Bertie reminded him, "if William hadn't got the half-crown by eight o'clock and he hasn't and it's eight now."

"All right," said Victor; "I'll go an' get it."

He disappeared into the house.

The village clock began to strike eight. One . . . two . . . three . . . four . . . five . . . six . . . seven . . .

At the seventh stroke Victor appeared with the football.

At the seventh stroke, too, something else happened.

A human tornado swept up the drive from the gate, snatched the football from Victor's hands and thrust a half-crown into them instead.

The eighth stroke struck.

William sank upon the top step, clasping his football closely to him.

"Crumbs!" he panted. "Only just in time!"

# Chapter 6

# William the Sleep-Maker

The whole thing began with Aunt Jane. Aunt Jane had been suffering from a nervous breakdown, and after a few weeks at a rest cure home had invited herself to the Browns' for a short visit before returning to normal life. William, though disliking aunts in general, was prepared to be interested in Aunt Jane. He had never met anyone before suffering from a nervous breakdown, and inquiries among his friends had led him to expect startling eccentricities of behaviour.

"They carry on same as if they were mad," Ginger informed him. "They're jus' *'xactly* like lunatics. . . ."

"No, they don't," Douglas contradicted. "I know 'cause our cook once knew one an' I asked her what they were like an' she said that they laugh an' cry all day long—first one then the other."

"Gosh!" said William, deeply impressed by the picture this description called up. "They must be rather jolly."

"No, they don't do that," said Henry. "They throw things about. I know 'cause I met a boy that knew one. They don't laugh or cry or carry on mad or anything like that. They jus' throw things about."

From this discussion was evolved a game in which William, Ginger, and Henry were "nervous breakdowners", and Douglas the proprietor of a "rest cure home".

The game developed into a very enjoyable fight in which all four of them—Douglas especially—received minor but picturesque injuries.

"What exactly *is* a rest cure home anyway?" demanded Ginger as he moved his tie from the back of his neck and retrieved the collar end that had slipped the moorings of its stud.

"It's a place where no one does any work," explained Henry.

"Gosh!" said William. "I'd jolly well like to go to one of them."

"They don't let you in unless you've got a nervous breakdown," said Henry.

"I bet it's easy to learn to act as if you had," said William. "I'm jolly well going to try anyway. I'm goin' to watch my aunt an' learn to carry on same as she does."

"You'll let us watch her too, won't you?" pleaded Ginger.

"All right," said William generously. "She's coming to-morrow night an' you can all come an' watch her carryin' on through the window first thing if you like."

They thanked him gratefully and were ready at their appointed stations outside the Browns' drawing-room window on the night of Aunt Jane's arrival. But Aunt Jane proved to be disappointingly normal. She did not throw things about or laugh or cry or behave in any way unlike the most ordinary person. William was apologetic for the failure of his exhibit.

"P'raps she's just tired to-night," he said to the disappointed and rather resentful audience. "She may be all right to-morrow."

But Aunt Jane remained exasperatingly normal even the next morning.

"Seems to me she's jus' like anyone else," William

muttered aggrievedly to his mother.

"Well, of course she is, dear," replied his mother, somewhat mystified.

"I thought she'd got one of those things—you know— that makes people act mad."

"A nervous breakdown! She had one, dear, but she's much better now. And anyway it only made her feel depressed. She was quite normal otherwise."

William, on hearing this, would have lost interest completely in Aunt Jane, had it not been for Aunt Jane's sleeping-draught. For at lunch that day Aunt Jane began to enlarge upon the symptoms of her nervous break- down, and after describing her insomnia at great length, said that she had taken a sleeping-draught every night for months. "I hardly ever use it now," she said, "but at one time I simply couldn't sleep without it. I would lie awake all night if I didn't have it. One dose used to send me off."

It so happened that the idea of a dose to induce sleep was a wholly novel one to William. The only difficulty he himself had experienced in that connection was in awakening from sleep or remaining awake when roused. He had invented many devices to ensure this on occa- sions when he and the Outlaws had arranged an early morning meeting in the woods, and all had been only partially successful.

The news, when handed on to the other Outlaws, was received with gratifying interest. Like William they had never before come in contact with the idea.

"I say," said Ginger, "wouldn't it be fun to put it in the pudding at school dinner an' watch everyone goin' off to sleep?"

"Gosh, yes!" said William, "an' we'd choose maths afternoon."

"An' Latin afternoon," put in Douglas.

"Why not every afternoon?" said Henry. "I say, I wonder if they know they've been to sleep when they wake up? Wouldn't it be fun to send them all to sleep every afternoon\an' let 'em wake up at four an' never know they'd not had lessons. An' we wouldn't take the stuff, of course. We'd jus' watch 'em all fall asleep an' then go out. We'd be able to have a holiday every afternoon then."

The others, while approving unreservedly of the plan, suspected that its details might prove more difficult to work out than appeared at first sight.

"We'd have to start on somethin' small at first," said William, "jus' to try it. But anyway we've not got any of the stuff yet an' I don't suppose we're likely to."

The next day, however, Aunt Jane announced at breakfast that she now slept so well without her sleeping-draught that she thought she'd be able to manage without it altogether.

William, who was consumed by a desire at least to see the mysterious potion, waited till his aunt had set off for the short walk ordered by her doctor, then furtively entered her bedroom and peeped into the well-stocked medicine chest that accompanied her everywhere. There it was—a small, innocent-looking bottle labelled "Sleeping-Draught". William gazed at it fascinated, again calling up the pleasant mental vision of the whole school (except the four Outlaws) slumbering away the hours sacred to maths and Latin under its effect. It was, of course, he admitted to himself, a vision impossible of attainment. There wasn't enough stuff in the bottle, for one thing. Reluctantly he was about to replace it when the idea of showing it to the other Outlaws occurred to him.

It wouldn't do any harm for them just to *see* it, he reasoned with himself. They were as deeply interested in it as he was, and it wouldn't be fair not to let them just *see* it. . . . He slipped it into his pocket and went to the Outlaws, who were waiting for him by his front gate.

"I say," he hissed in his most conspiratorial whisper, "come into the summer-house. I've got that stuff to show you."

Eagerly they followed him. With rapt and breathless interest they gazed at the small bottle he held in his hand.

"There's not enough to do the whole school," said William regretfully, "but—let's jus' try a little of it. Jus' such a little she'll never miss it. Who'll have a bit jus' to try?"

But it appeared that none of the Outlaws wished to undergo the treatment. All of them wished instead to watch the effect of the treatment on someone else. As Ginger said, "if you're the one goin' to sleep you miss all the fun."

"Let's draw lots," said William. But this, too, the Outlaws refused to do. They were not going to run the risk of being chosen for the lot of sleeping-partner.

"*Tell* you what!" said William when the *impasse* seemed to be assuming the proportions of an insolvable problem. "I'll go'n' get one of my white rats an' we'll give it some an' watch it go to sleep. . . ."

He departed and soon reappeared with a white rat in each hand and a third in his pocket.

Some of the mixture was poured upon a little bread; of which the rats eagerly partook. With gratifying promptness they then lay down, overcome apparently by sleep. The Outlaws watched eagerly.

"Gosh!" said Ginger. "It jolly well acts all right, doesn't it?"

"I say," said William, "wouldn't it be jolly fine if we had enough to send everyone in the world to sleep except ourselves? We'd make a sort of gas of it an' shoot it out an' we'd wear masks so as we shouldn't go to sleep, an' everyone else in the world would be asleep an' I bet we'd have some fun. All the shopmen would be asleep an' we'd be able to jus' take what we wanted out of the shops an' all the policemen would be asleep so that no one could put us in prison an' all the school-masters would be asleep so that we couldn't have school an'— well, I bet we'd have a *jolly* good time."

"I wonder how long they sleep," said Ginger thoughtfully, looking at the still unconscious forms of the white rats.

"Let's try'n' wake 'em," said Douglas, and proceeded to shout "Hi!" loudly in the ears of the limp white bodies.

"No," he said at last, discontinuing his efforts for want of breath, "it must be jolly good stuff. Nothin' seems to wake 'em."

"Let's try'n' find somethin' else to do it on," said William, who was longing once again to try the effect of the potent mixture. "Ginger and me'll stop here an' watch for when the rats wake up an' you two go an' bring somethin' else."

"What'll we bring?" demanded Douglas.

"Well, don't bring anythin' too big," said William. "Not a cow or a horse or anythin' like that. There's not very much left in the bottle an' anyway they take up so much room an' I'd get into an awful row if they found I'd got cows or horses sleepin' in the summer-house."

In less than ten minutes the scouts had returned with a stray cat—a mangy, bony creature, ragged of ear and fierce of eye.

"Give it some quick," gasped Douglas, who was carrying on a losing struggle with his unwilling captive. "It's half killed me, an' I can't hold it a minute longer.

We found it nosing in a dustbin."

William dashed into the house and returned with a saucer of milk. He was only just in time, as the cat was merely staying to administer a few final and well-

THE CAT LAPPED GREEDILY, WHILE THE OUTLAWS STOOD ROUND WATCHING WITH BATED BREATH.

directed scratches on Ginger's face before making off. But at sight of the milk it paused in the work and its gaunt eyes gleamed exultantly. It sprang from Ginger's arms and streaked across the floor of the summer-house to where William had set down the saucer. It lapped greedily for some moments while the Outlaws stood round watching with bated breath. Then it looked up, staggered a few paces from the saucer, and collapsed. William lifted its unconscious form and placed it on the seat of the summer-house next to the rats.

He stood looking down at the motionless row.

"Gosh!" he said again, in an awestruck voice. "It jolly well makes them sleep all right, doesn't it?"

\* \* \*

The Outlaws arrived at William's house early next morning to see if the sleepers had yet awakened. But the three rats and the mangy cat still lay limp and motionless on the summer-house seat. So literal-minded were the Outlaws that it never occurred to them that the unconsciousness could be anything but sleep. The bottle was labelled "Sleeping-Draught", therefore it must produce sleep and nothing more.

"Let's try 'n' wake 'em up again," suggested William, and again the Outlaws placed their mouths to the ears of their victims and shouted "Hi!" till they were hoarse. Proddings with a stick produced no better results.

"I say, I wish we could do ole Markie," said Ginger, looking down wistfully at the limp forms. "I jolly well wish we could make him sleep as long as this. Then there couldn't be any school."

"Yes, there would," said William. "They'd jus' send another headmaster down to carry on till he woke up."

"Then we'd do *him*," said Ginger.

William glanced down at the half-empty bottle.

"No," he said sadly; "there's not enough to go on doing people like that."

William, as a matter of fact, was beginning to feel slightly conscience-stricken about the sleeping-draught. He had taken it without permission and, carried away by scientific interest in his experiments, had already used so much that his aunt could not fail to notice it. So conspicuous indeed would be the fact of the drug's having been tampered with that William decided not to replace the bottle in his aunt's medicine chest. Better that his aunt should think she had mislaid the bottle than that she should know that someone else had been using it. He hid it at the bottom of his handkerchief drawer and watched his aunt warily, ready to assume at once his expression of dreamy innocence should she mention the disappearance of the bottle. The disappearance, however, remained undiscovered, Aunt Jane only referring to the matter indirectly by remarking that she was still sleeping so well as to have no need of her draught. Meantime the sleepers in the summer-house continued to sleep.

"Gosh!" said William more than once. "Won't they be jolly well surprised when they wake up! I say, I bet they'll think it's three days ago still, won't they? They'll feel jolly muddled!"

Henry complained of an unpleasant smell in the summer-house, but the others denied it with asperity.

"You've got smells on the brain," William informed him indignantly. "What could smell here anyway?"

"I think it's that cat," suggested Henry mildly.

"Well, we know it wasn't a clean cat," admitted William. "You found it in a dustbin, didn't you? But I'm not goin' to start washin' it now it's asleep. It would prob'ly wake up an' start goin' for me. If you want it washed you can jolly well do it yourself."

Henry, however, forbore to avail himself of this permission, and the subject of the smell was dropped.

William's mother would, of course, have realised from William's expression that he was engaged upon some secret and in all probability lawless activity, had not her whole attention been taken up by the visit of Mr. Forrester. Mr. Forrester was coming to preside over the annual concert of the local Temperance Society and to say a few words on temperance before the concert began. The Vicar's wife had arranged for the visit of Mr. Forrester, but with characteristic adroitness had arranged for him to dine with the Browns.

"But why?" demanded Mr. Brown wildly when his wife broke the news to him. "Why should he dine with us? That woman's asked him to come. Why shouldn't she give him his dinner?"

"I think, dear," said Mrs. Brown mildly, "it's because the Vicar likes a glass of wine to his dinner and Mr. Forrester's in favour of total abstinence."

"Well, I like a glass of wine to my dinner, too," said Mr. Brown indignantly.

"I'm sorry, dear," said Mrs. Brown, "but I somehow didn't realise what she was doing till she'd done it and—well, I really *daren't* have any wine on the table. You must just do without it for that night. He's the most famous speaker on total abstinence in the whole movement."

Mr. Brown groaned again, but yielded to the inevitable.

"Oh, well," he said, "I suppose it will soon be over. But next time it happens," he threatened darkly, "I'll run away to sea."

Mr. Forrester proved to be a large and talkative man. He gave the appearance of having been wound up for his public addresses to such an extent that he never had time to run down between them. He had a pompous platform manner even when merely saying that he'd have another cup of tea. William was rather distrait and did not take his usual interest in the visitor. His thoughts were absorbed by the sleeping-draught. He was oppressed by a sense of guilt at having purloined it and yet he was tormented by an intense desire to use it again. He felt that he would know no peace till he had again watched the fascinating spectacle of something falling asleep under its influence. He was tired of rats and cats. He wanted to try it on a human being, yet from this his conscience restrained him. He had taken it without permission. It was very expensive stuff (he had heard his aunt dilating more than once on the expensiveness of it). He ought not to use it at all. He certainly ought not to waste it. Absorbed by this problem, he took so long washing his hands and brushing his hair that he was late for dinner on the night of the guest's arrival. As he entered the room Mr. Forrester was describing his zeal in the cause of total abstinence.

"I think I may truly say," he was remarking, "that in this good work I never sleep. Never, never sleep."

William entered the room just in time to catch the last part of this statement. "I never sleep. Never, never sleep."

William's attention was, of course, immediately aroused. He accepted quite literally the fact that Mr. Forrester never slept. Then surely someone ought to help him to sleep. Often had William heard his aunt describing the evils that attended lack of sleep. His spirits rose. It would not be wasting the precious stuff to use it on Mr. Forrester. It was, on the contrary, his clear duty to use it on Mr. Forrester. He would be saving Mr. Forrester from a nervous breakdown, perhaps from madness. It only remained to find some opportunity to administer the saving drug, but he had not long to wait for that.

"Water, I suppose, Mr. Forrester?" said Mrs. Brown.

"Well," said Mr. Forrester, clearing his throat as if for a long and eloquent address, "if you *have* some ginger-ale . . ."

"Oh, yes . . . " said Mrs. Brown. "I believe there's a case in the cellar."

She was putting her finger on the bell when William sprang to his feet.

"I'll get it," he said eagerly.

WILLIAM SEEMED TO TAKE A LONG TIME FETCHING THE GINGER-ALE, AND WHEN IT FINALLY APPEARED IT WAS IN A GLASS.

"Good boy!" said Mr. Forrester approvingly. "I always like to see a child ready and willing to save other people trouble."

Mr. and Mrs. Brown tried somewhat unsuccessfully to look as if this were the normal character of their son, and William hurried out of the room before they had recovered from their efforts.

William seemed to take a long time fetching the ginger-ale, and when it finally appeared it was in a glass.

"Thank you, my dear boy," boomed Mr. Forrester as William set the glass by him, "thank you very much."

He noticed that the ginger-ale had a rather peculiar taste and that the boy who had so kindly fetched it for him watched him through the meal with embarrassing intensity. All that Mr. and Mrs. Brown noticed was a merciful diminishing of their guest's eloquence. The guest himself seemed to be aware of this and to make strenuous efforts to fight against it. He glanced once or twice at the windows, but they were open. Odd that he felt so drowsy all of a sudden. . . .

"Well," said Mrs. Brown at last, rising, "I suppose we ought to be making our way to the Village Hall."

Mr. Forrester went into the hall, put on his coat, and set off with Mrs. Brown, Aunt Jane and William to the Village Hall. He was strangely silent on the way. At the door of the Village Hall he shook hands with the Vicar and the Vicar's wife in a dazed, bewildered fashion.

"They're just ready for your speech," said the Vicar.

"Yes," said Mr. Forrester, "yes, yes, yes," but his voice had lost its famous resonance and—a strange thing for him—he spoke rather than boomed.

"This way," said the Vicar.

Mr. Forrester found himself upon the platform. Just beneath him in the front row sat the boy who had brought him the ginger-ale, still gazing at him with that peculiar intensity. It was all very odd. Again Mr. Forrester glanced at the window to see if any closeness of the atmosphere could account for the drowsiness that was stealing over him so irresistibly. But these windows, too, were open. The clapping that had greeted his appearance was dying down. He made a strenuous effort to throw off the drowsiness. He took his notes out of his pocket.

"LADIES AND GENTLEMEN," HE BEGAN, "ON MY WAY HERE I PASSED THE WHITE LION."

"Ladies and gentlemen——" he began. The notes slid from his hands on to the floor. Someone picked them up. He took them as firmly as he could in both hands, but again they slid to the floor. They were handed to him again, and he put them on to the table. After all, he didn't really need them. He always made the same speech and he knew it by heart.

He always began by saying: "On the way here I passed"—naming the local public-house—"and I thought to myself . . . " and there followed a dissertation on the number of such institutions, and the damage caused by each drink sold in each. He had at least managed to notice the name of the public-house on his way from the Browns' house to the Village Hall.

He began his speech with an effort.

"Ladies and Gentlemen," he repeated, "on my way here I passed The White Lion." Here he swayed and put his hand to his brow. "The White Lion," he repeated bemusedly. "I passed the White Lion——"

Suddenly he sat down, laid his head on the table and murmuring once more, "The White Lion" fell into what had every appearance of being a drunken stupor. There were sounds of consternation from the expensive seats in the front, ribald laughter from the cheap ones at the back.

The village doctor made his way up from the body of the hall and pronounced that the lecturer ought to go to bed at once.

"You'll put him up, won't you, dear?" said the Vicar's wife to Mrs. Brown, and before Mrs. Brown could protest had summoned a taxi and given the driver the Browns' address. The doctor helped the Vicar to carry the unconscious temperance enthusiast to the taxi and set off with him, accompanied by Mrs. Brown and Aunt Jane, who was loudly threatening an immediate return to her nervous breakdown. Mr. Brown, disturbed by their premature return, slipped his whisky and soda into the sideboard cupboard and came out to watch the still unconscious form of Mr. Forrester being carried out of the cab.

"Good Lord," he said, "what's happened?"

"I think he's drunk," said Mrs. Brown wildly. "He just began his speech on total abstinence and then went off like this."

The doctor and Mr. Brown carried their guest upstairs, assisted by William, who had now appeared on the scene, wearing his famous expression of dreamy innocence. Aunt Jane was describing at great length the effect that the evening's catastrophe had had on her nervous system and anounced her intention of taking a strong dose of her sleeping-draught and going straight to bed.

The doctor, having examined his patient, came down to say that he was suffering from an overdose of narcotic, but would soon be all right.

"A pity!" said the doctor, shaking his head. "The last man one would expect to be a secret drug addict."

At this point Aunt Jane entered the room. Aunt Jane was in what is generally described as a "state". She said that her sleeping-draught had disappeared. She said that that meant she wouldn't sleep a wink. She said her nervous breakdown would return, and, in fact, she felt it returning already. She said that if she'd had any idea that there would be all these goings-on she'd never have come and she did think that someone ought to have warned her. She was obviously capable of continuing in this strain indefinitely. William had crept out of the room at the beginning of it. Half-way through it Mr. Brown also took his departure. Aunt Jane continued to expatiate to her diminished audience—now consisting of the doctor and Mrs. Brown—on the symptoms and history of her nervous breakdown. Before she had come to the end of it, Mr. Brown reappeared. He carried the empty bottle of sleeping-draught which he had found in the pocket of William's overcoat in the hall. William had put it there for safety after emptying its contents into the ginger-ale.

Some instinct (not wholly unconnected with the sense of smell) had also led Mr. Brown to the summer-house.

"I think," said Mr. Brown grimly as he entered the room, "that the mystery is solved. Mr. Forrester is not the only drug addict on the premises. The others are a cat and three rats. These have taken a fatal dose. Mr. Forrester on the whole may consider himself lucky. . . . " He rang the bell and said to the housemaid with undiminished grimness: "Send Master William to me, please."

"Master William's gone out, sir," said the house-maid.

"Well, he'll come back—unfortunately," said Mr. Brown, "and I'll deal with him when he does."

"Yes, but what's *happened*?" demanded Mrs. Brown, as soon as she could spare time from Aunt Jane, whose emotion at sight of her empty bottle had reached a fine pitch of hysteria that had demanded the full attention of both Mrs. Brown and the doctor. "Who's responsible for all this?"

"William is, my dear," said her husband.

Mrs. Brown sighed resignedly.

"I suppose we might have known. . . . " she said.

# Chapter 7

# William and the Russian Prince

The Brown household was moved to its depths when Robert received an invitation to the cricket week at Marleigh Manor. For Marleigh Manor—unlike most of the large houses in the neighbourhood, which were now inhabited by wholly successful if only partly educated tradesmen—was a stronghold of aristocracy, and its cricket week was a social event.

Robert paled on reading his invitation.

"But, good heavens!" he gasped. "I shan't know what to do. I mean—well, you know, I simply shan't know what to *do*."

"Why not, darling?" said Mrs. Brown. (Mrs. Brown was the sort of mother who could not imagine her children at a disadvantage in any circumstances whatsoever.) "You play cricket so nicely."

"I know I do," said Robert modestly, "but that's not the point. A *week*. Butlers and footmen and that sort of thing. And people with titles. I—well, I shan't know what to *do*."

"Nonsense, dear," said Mrs. Brown. "All you have to do is to be just your own natural self."

But Robert had less faith in his own natural self than Mrs. Brown had.

"It's all very well to say that," he rejoined gloomily,

"but—I shan't know what to *do*. I mean, half the people there will have valets."

William's face lit up.

"I say," he said eagerly, "s'pose I go with Robert and pretend to be his valet."

"Nonsense, dear!" said Mrs. Brown.

"I'll go as his butler, then," said William. "Honest, they'd think a lot more of him bringin' his butler with him. I bet all the high-up people take their butlers with them when they go to stay at places."

"Nonsense, dear!" said Mrs. Brown again.

"If you come within a mile of the place while I'm staying there," said Robert savagely, "I'll wring your neck."

"All right," said William distantly, "I was only tryin' to help you. That's all I was tryin' to do. I'd make a jolly fine butler. So don't blame me if no one takes any notice of you there."

"No, I won't," said Robert, and added bitterly: "And I don't want the sort of notice people take of me when you're anywhere about. I've had enough of that to last a lifetime, thank you very much."

"Now, children, don't quarrel," said Mrs. Brown mildly; "there's a lot to arrange if Robert's going. Perhaps you ought to have a new white waistcoat for your dress-suit, ought you, dear?"

William walked away, leaving them to an animated discussion of Robert's wardrobe.

For the next few days he preserved an aloof attitude, an attitude that said more plainly than words that he had given Robert his chance and Robert had not taken it, therefore Robert could now stew in his own juice. But he was not really as aloof as he appeared. Secretly he was deeply interested in this opening of the strongholds of aristocracy to Robert and anxious to do something to further Robert's prestige within them.

"Couldn't I go as his page if he won't take a butler?" he said to Mrs. Brown.

"Don't be so silly, William," said Mrs. Brown patiently. "People don't have pages nowadays."

"Well, it might start a fashion and make him famous," retorted William.

"Nonsense, dear!" said Mrs. Brown.

"Which is highest," said William, after a pause, "Sir or Duke?"

"Duke. Why?"

"Well, I thought I'd write to Robert while he was there and put Sir Robert Brown or Duke Robert Brown on the envelope; whichever's the highest. Or what about Earl?"

"William, you mustn't do anything of the *sort*," said Mrs. Brown, aghast. "Robert would be *furious*."

"Well, I can't think why. If it was me goin' there I'd arrange with someone to do that while I was there. I wouldn't mind paying someone to do that—to send me a letter every day with Duke or Earl on. If Robert wasn't so mean he'd give me a sixpence a letter for doing it. And then I'd put Buckingham Palace, London, on it too, and cross it out as if he'd been staying with the King an' was havin' his letters sent on from there. Seems to me Robert hasn't got any sense. If it was me I'd have them all thinkin' I was the most high-up person there by the end of a day. I'd be spendin' all the time now writin' envelopes like that for people to post to me 'stead of fussin' 'cause there's a patch on one pair of pyjamas, and the stripes go the wrong way on the other, like what Robert's doing."

"I'm making him a new pair of pyjamas," said Mrs. Brown apologetically. "It's only in one sleeve that the stripes go the wrong way. I was using up an odd bit of stuff and really I can't see even now that it matters so terribly. However——" The "however" evidently meant that tirades of eloquence from the nervous Robert had convinced her that it did.

"After all," she ended, "it's very good flannel, and personally I don't think anyone would notice that the stripes go the wrong way on just that one sleeve."

"Why don't you embroider coats of arms and things on his clothes?" said William thoughtfully. "That would make him seem more high-up. I bet all high-up people have coats of arms an' things embroidered all over their clothes."

"Nonsense, dear!" said Mrs. Brown once more.

"Seems to me," said William bitterly, "no one wants to help Robert but me. You won't let me go as his page or his butler or send him high-up letters, an' you won't even embroider coats of arms an' things on his clothes. Well, I've done my best and I hope you won't blame me if no one takes any notice of him there."

Mrs. Brown promised that she wouldn't, and William relapsed into an offended silence.

He watched Robert morosely when the fateful day arrived, and Robert, looking pale and nervous and carrying his suit-case, set off to walk the few miles that separated his home from Marleigh Manor.

"I don't expect that anyone'll even *speak* to him," he muttered despondently. "'Tisn't even as if he *looked* high-up. An' if he'd let me help he'd've had 'em all callin' him Your Royal Highness an' suchlike as soon as he got there."

When a day had passed without news of Robert, William's curiosity became more than he could endure, and he set off by a circuitous route to Marleigh Manor. Cricket was in full swing on the cricket field, and William crept along in the ditch till he was just behind the bench

"NO ONE WANTS TO HELP ROBERT BUT ME," SAID WILLIAM
BITTERLY. "YOU WON'T LET ME GO AS HIS BUTLER, AND YOU
WON'T EVEN EMBROIDER COATS OF ARMS ON HIS CLOTHES."

where he could see Robert sitting watching the game.
On two wicker chairs some distance from the bench sat
Lady Markham, the chatelaine of Marleigh Manor, and
by her side a hook-nosed crony armed with a *lorgnette*.

"My dear," Lady Markham was saying, "I simply
don't know who half the people are who are staying in
the house. One doesn't nowadays. My husband meets a
man in a train—in a *train*, mind you—who's interested in
old coins—my husband has a *wonderful* collection, you
know—and promptly asks him over for the week. He's
all *right*, of course. A charming man. And he's brought
his secretary with him. He's writing a book on old coins
and the secretary's taking notes and making sketches of

my husband's collection. But really, you know, when I was young, people simply didn't ask casual acquaintances to their houses without knowing anything about their families. And half the young men Ronnie's asked for the cricket I've never seen before, and never even *heard* of their people."

William passed on noiselessly in his ditch. Sir Gerald Markham sat a short distance away next to a grey-bearded, benevolent-looking old man who was evidently the coin enthusiast.

"Of course," Sir Gerald was saying, "no coins compare in interest with the Roman coins. I have, I believe, one of the earliest in existence. They weren't struck at all, you know, under the Empire. . . . "

William moved on to where Robert sat rather forlornly at the end of the bench. Next to him was a youthful beauty of the peroxide blonde type and a tall youth with dark curling hair. The two of them were evidently engrossed in each other. And Robert was as evidently attracted by the blonde beauty, who seemed, for her part, unaware of his existence. William took in the whole situation at a glance. He had not been Robert's brother for eleven years for nothing. His heart burnt for Robert, thus neglected and ignored. It was his own fault, of course. If Robert had only taken him as butler or page, if Robert had that morning received a letter addressed to Earl Robert Brown and apparently forwarded from Buckingham Palace, if he had been able even now carelessly to draw up his trouser leg and reveal the top of his sock embroidered with a coat of arms, the attitude of the blonde beauty, William knew, would be very different. It was Robert's own fault, and yet William felt it his duty to extricate him, if possible, from the morass of nonentity and neglect into which he seemed to have landed himself. He crept away, his brow knitted, his freckled face wearing an expression of grim purposefulness. He must go very carefully, of course. Robert must know nothing of his efforts. If Robert knew of them he would certainly do his best to thwart them, so obstinate and pig-headed was he even when it was a question of his own good.

William went to his back garden, sat on an upturned flower-pot, his chin in his hand, the faithful Jumble lying by his side, and unavailingly racked his brains for a plan. At last he gave up the attempt in despair and, fetching the penny shocker that he had begun in bed last night (the keyhole stuffed with cotton wool, the mat pressed tightly up against the door, to hide all traces of the crime), lay down at full length on the lawn and went on with it.

And the penny shocker, as if to repay him for the risks he had run on its behalf, gave him his plan.

\* \* \*

The blonde beauty—whose name, by the way, was Clarinda Bellew—walked slowly down the field towards the wood that bordered it. It happened that all the eligible and good-looking youths of the party were playing cricket, and she was feeling bored. She was tired of hearing her host dilating on his unique collection of coins and her hostess lamenting the deterioration in the manners and deportment of the young since the days of her own youth.

She was passing the point where the wood joined the field when she heard a loud cough and turned with a start to meet the fixed stare of a small boy crouching behind a bush.

"What are you doing here?" she said haughtily.

"I'm on guard," he said.

"On guard?" she repeated, impressed despite herself

by the unflinching earnestness of the small boy's gaze. He was obviously no youthful trespasser caught red-handed.

"Yes. . . . There's a Russian prince playin' cricket with those people an' I've been told by Scotland Yard to guard him."

"WHAT ARE YOU DOING HERE?" SHE SAID HAUGHTILY. "I'M ON GUARD," SAID WILLIAM.

"You!" The blonde beauty struggled with her amazement. "But why you?"

"Well, you see," said William, "they thought that no one would think it funny to see a boy hanging round watching a cricket match, but a policeman or plain-clothes man would make people sort of suspicious. I'm a good deal older than what I look, of course. I've been kept small by Scotland Yard so as to be able to take on jobs like this. Anyway, I'm supposed to be watchin' this Russian prince to see no harm comes to him."

Clarinda's blue eyes had grown wider and wider during this recital. Like William she fed largely on sensational fiction. Moreover, she was a regular attendant at the "pictures". Such a situation as William described was nothing to the situations that she swallowed daily without question on the films or in novels. And William's frowning purposeful gaze was almost hypnotic in its convincingness.

"Which one is it?" said Clarinda wonderingly.

William looked over to where the game was going on.

"It's that one . . . the one that's batting now."

They both gazed at the unconscious Robert for a few moments in silence.

"B-b-but," stammered Clarinda, amazed, bewildered, deeply intrigued, "I thought that he was someone who lived over in the next village."

William laughed—a short grim laugh.

"Oh, yes, that's what he's *supposed* to be," he said. "He was rescued from the revolution when he was a boy and brought over here secret and given to this family to pretend he was their son so as to keep him in hiding. You see"—William's voice sank to a sinister whisper—"you see, the Bolshevists are after him. He got away with all his jewels for one thing, and they're after his jewels." He warmed to his subject as a fresh and thrilling idea occurred to him. "You see that very dark man over there?" and he pointed to the youth who had engrossed the maiden's whole attention to the exclusion of poor Robert the day before.

"Yes," she said excitedly, "it's Theo Horner."

"Well, he's a Bolshevist. He's after the jewels. That's why I'm told to guard this Russian prince against him."

"But what could you do?" she said, looking down at his small stocky figure.

He assumed a mysterious expression.

"Oh, I've got ways," he said. "I've got secret signals. I could have all Scotland Yard here in no time if I gave some of my secret signals."

His eyes met hers unflinchingly, and the last of her doubts disappeared. After all, she'd always believed that things like this were happening all round one all the time if only one knew where to look for them. Life couldn't really be as dull as it seemed on the surface. All the thrills couldn't really be confined to the cinema. Well, here was one in real life—a thrill as big as any she'd ever seen on the pictures.

The situation resolved itself quite simply in her mind into the usual triangle—herself the heroine, Robert the hero, Theo the villain. She gazed reflectively at Robert, who—an agile figure in white flannels—was running across the pitch after hitting the ball clear of the fielders.

"One might have known," she said dreamily. "He looks an aristocrat. Every inch an aristocrat."

"You won't tell anyone, will you?" said William anxiously. "I mean—well, they'd probably get him at once if they knew anyone knew."

"Of course," said Clarinda, her very soul athrill. "Of course I quite understand that."

"You see," hissed William, "your life'll be in danger too if anyone finds out you know."

Clarinda closed her eyes in silent bliss. From the age of ten, when she had attended her first film, she had been longing for someone to say something like that to her.

"I'm not afraid," she said, making her eyes as big as possible and seeing an imaginary "close up" of her face wearing its proud brave smile. "I've never known what it is to be afraid."

"And most of all," William said, "you mustn't let him know you know."

"The prince?"

"Yes, the prince. If he knew you knew he'd go straight away an' none of us would ever see him again."

"No, of course I won't," she said, doing another imaginary "close up" even better than the first—a "close up" in which the dreamy gaze of dawning love was mingled with the proud brave smile. She already saw herself as a Russian princess, loaded with jewels of fabulous value. She would be deeply involved in international plots. By a daring *coup*, which would make her one of the most famous figures in history, she would overthrow the Soviet and restore her husband to the throne.

When she awoke from this dazzling vision she found herself alone. The small boy had disappeared. She walked back to the others in a slightly dazed condition. It *had* happened, of course? It wasn't all a dream? That small boy hadn't been pulling her leg? No . . . she recalled his earnest face, his determined frown. No, he couldn't have been pulling her leg. The story sounded impossible, but not half as impossible as things that had actually happened in history and were printed in black and white in history books. Not to speak of the films. . . .

Robert was surprised to be greeted by her with a dazzling smile when he returned from the cricket pitch. Theo was equally surprised to be greeted with cold indifference.

"Do come for a little stroll with me," she said to Robert, fixing her blue eyes upon him. "One gets so stiff just hanging about."

"I'd love to," said Robert.

She drew a deep breath.

How courtly his manners were, how princely his bearing! She might have guessed. . . .

Robert was slightly distrait, which, of course, added greatly to the air of mystery with which Clarinda had already invested him. What was he thinking about? she wondered. About the princely surroundings of his childhood, which, of course, he could not have forgotten? About the dangers among which he now moved? About the great *coup* that might restore to him his fallen fortunes? As a matter of fact, Robert was thinking about the entertainment that the cricket eleven was to give to the rest of the house party at the week-end. One item was to be a skit on Hamlet, and Robert had been chosen to represent Hamlet. He had been given a script of his part to learn and had been sworn to the utmost secrecy on the subject. It was a point of honour with the Marleigh Manor Cricket Team that no single piece of information about their programme should leak out before the actual performance. They boasted that in all the years that they had been holding the cricket week with its grand finale of the dramatic entertainment, the programme had never leaked out yet.

"They'll all try to worm it out of you," they had warned Robert, "but keep your mouth shut about it whatever you do."

Robert had kept his mouth shut about it, but he was nevertheless feeling guilty and ill at ease, for he had left the script of his part in the library that morning for over an hour and was terrified that someone might have come in and read it. He had rushed back to retrieve it as soon as he had discovered its loss and had found it just where he had left it, but—suppose someone had been in the interval and seen it and already the news was common property? At the thought that it might be he who had broken the tradition of years, completely disgracing himself by his carelessness, the perspiration broke out on his brow. Clarinda thrilled as she watched the obvious signs of his uneasiness and mental distress. So should a man look who carries his life in his hands, a man surrounded on all sides by his own enemies and the enemies of his race. It was all eminently satisfactory. Suddenly she decided to let him know that he had at least one friend in the network of foes that surrounded him. She laid her hand on his arm.

"Don't look so worried . . . Prince," she said.

The blood flamed into his face. She knew. She knew that he was to be Hamlet. She'd been into the library and read his script. The others would never forgive him. He was disgraced for ever.

"You know?" he gasped.

"Yes, I know," she said sweetly.

"You . . . I say, you haven't told anyone, have you?"

"No. Not a soul," she assured him with the ravishing smile.

Poor boy, how young he looked to live this life of constant deadly danger.

"You—you won't tell a soul, will you?" he pleaded. "I mean—well, I shall be simply *ruined* if you do."

"I know," she said. "I know all about it. You can rely on me. I shan't tell a soul. And I'll never mention it again even to you."

But she couldn't resist adding: "Have you got the jewels with you here?"

It so happened that Hamlet's outfit included a large amount of "jewellery" that had been purchased for the occasion at the Woolworth's branch of the neighbouring country town.

"Yes," answered Robert innocently. "I've got them upstairs in my bedroom."

Clarinda closed her eyes and drew a deep breath of

ecstasy. It was all too marvellously, marvellously film-like. She decided to tackle Theo, too, before the day was out. Just hint to him that she knew what he was up to . . . not to say anything definite, of course.

She found him after tea reading a novel on a wicker chair on the terrace. He put down his novel and sprang to his feet eagerly.

"I say," he said, "come for a walk with me, will you?"

She took up his novel, opened the fly-leaf and read the name, "Theodore Horner."

"I wonder what you'd say," she said slowly, "if I told you that I *knew* your name wasn't really Theodore Horner."

The blood flamed hotly into the young man's face, and he shifted his eyes from hers in unmistakable guilt. Since the day he went to a public school he had been striving to hide from his contemporaries the fact that the name Theo by which he was known was short, not for Theodore, but for Theodosius. He had inadvertently revealed this fact at his prep school, and his life there had been in consequence a protracted persecution. Learning wisdom from that, he had always afterwards pretended that his name was Theodore. But now this girl had evidently discovered the truth, and there were plenty of people at the house party who could, he knew, make the name the theme of unending witticisms. And he was a dignified young man, who disliked being ragged.

Clarinda gazed at him sternly.

"Well?" she said.

"Don't tell anyone, will you?" he pleaded.

"No," she said, "I've already promised not to do that. But—remember I know, that's all."

With that she turned on her heel and left him.

But the deep glance she had sent from her blue eyes

before she left him increased his enslavement. She knew that his name was Theodosius, but she'd promised not to tell, and she wasn't the sort of girl to rag one, so it was all right. . . . She was *jolly* pretty, and she'd really seemed quite to take to him. He'd ask her to go for a walk with him before dinner. He went in search of her and found her playing a single with Robert. She played with Robert till dinner-time and after dinner danced with Robert till bedtime. The next day she and Robert were inseparable, and the bewildered Theo was snubbed unmercifully whenever he approached her. He couldn't understand it. She'd been simply ripping to him till she'd found that his name was Theodosius and then she'd changed suddenly and completely. It was jolly unfair. Theodosius was a potty name, but, after all, it wasn't his fault he'd been christened it. Girls, he decided not for the first time, were frightfully queer.

William, of course, hovered near to keep an eye on the very satisfactory results of his handiwork. Robert would have been surprised and horrified had he known how often his dallyings with the divine Clarinda were closely watched by William from the refuge of the ditch, or the bushes outside the window of the Manor. William was becoming bolder and bolder in his expeditions. He kept well out of Robert's way, and no one else seemed to take any notice of him. Once he ran full tilt into the benevolent-looking coin enthusiast as he was rounding a corner of the shrubbery. He assumed his mock fatuously imbecile expression and said:

"Please, sir, may I just look round the garden a bit?" and the benevolent-looking coin enthusiast had patted his head and replied benevolently:

"Certainly, my boy, look round as much as you like."

William treasured the permission as something to fall back upon in case of need.

He was delighted to see Robert basking in the favour of the blonde beauty, but there was no doubt that trouble was brewing from the quarter of the dispossessed suitor. For Theodosius had quickly passed from a state of bewilderment to one of aggrievement and from one of aggrievement to one of active resentment. This Brown fellow had simply pinched Clarinda from under his nose and flaunted his victory with open exultation. Well, he—Theodosius—wasn't the sort of chap to put up meekly with that sort of thing, and he'd jolly well *show* that Brown fellow so before he'd done with him. Every night in his dreams he pummelled poor Robert with monotonous regularity, and every day he followed Robert about with a ferocious scowl that made even Robert, uplifted as he was by Clarinda's sweetness, feel slightly nervous.

Clarinda herself, who now lived completely in the Russian-prince dream, accepted Theo's attitude quite simply as that of the Red Russian thirsting for the White Russian's blood—not to speak of his family jewels.

"You know," she said to Robert, "I do think you ought to be careful. He looked at you like murder then. Where do you keep them?"

"What?"

"The jewels."

"Oh, those." (Extraordinary how girls' minds could hop about from one subject to another.) "Oh, I've got them upstairs."

"Well, you *will* be careful, won't you?"

"Yes, rather! of course I will," promised Robert vaguely.

Then, because Robert's aristocratic birth belonged to the past and his possible conflict with his enemy to the future, and because, after all, the present was really more interesting than either, they fell to discussing the films they had seen recently and, by a natural process of reasoning, passed on to Clarinda's resemblance to the film stars whom Robert most admired. It was while they were engaged in this absorbing conversation that Theo passed and directed upon Robert a look so venomous that Clarinda felt something must be done at once to avert the tragedy that seemed to be threatening the exiled prince.

It was quite by chance that she ran into William, crouching in his hiding-place in the shrubbery waiting for an opportunity to approach the window and watch the progress of the situation he had so successfully created.

"Oh, there you are!" she said. "I was just wondering how to get hold of you. I say, you know, things are getting serious. I think you ought to *do* something. . . ."

"What can I do?" said William, taken off his guard for a minute.

"I thought you were in constant communication with Scotland Yard," said Clarinda.

"Yes, I am," agreed William hastily, "yes . . . yes, of course I am."

"I suppose you can communicate with them by wireless any time?" went on Clarinda, whose knowledge of wireless was rudimentary in the extreme, and who, in fact, imagined it to be some mystic means of communication independent of any instrument.

"Oh, yes," said William, "oh yes . . . I can do that all right."

"Well, do you know," she continued earnestly, "I really think you ought to be on the spot. I mean, you never saw anything like the way that villain's glaring at him. I do wish he hadn't got the jewels with him."

"Yes," agreed William, "I told him that was a mistake, but he was scared of leaving them anywhere else."

"Yes, of course, I quite understand that. But—well, I think that you ought to be on the spot, so as to be able to communicate with Scotland Yard at once in case of danger. You see, I'm frightened of to-night."

"Why?" said William. "Is it the play to-night?"

"No, that's to-morrow," said Clarinda, "and I'm not worrying about that. I don't even know whether the prince is in the play at all." (It thrilled her to say "the prince" casually like that.) "But to-night is the dance we're giving to the village cricket team in the barn, and we're having a little dance ourselves there first before they arrive, and—well, I'm nervous. I think the Bolshie may take the opportunity either to steal the jewels or to do something to the prince. I suppose there's a deadly vendetta between them!"

"Oh, yes," said William vaguely, "oh, yes, there's that all right."

"Well, I think you ought to be on the spot. Look here, how about telling Lady Markham everything and asking her advice?"

William's blood ran cold at this prospect.

"Oh, no," he said earnestly, "that would jolly well spoil everything. Rob—I mean the prince would go away at once if she knew. I mean, I've sworn to keep it secret, and if anyone finds I've told even you I'd prob'ly get put in prison for life, an' "—he sought for a more horrible prospect as Clarinda seemed unmoved by this— "an' prob'ly the prince'd get put to death by torcher."

She shuddered.

"Perhaps you're right," she said. "Perhaps we ought to go on keeping it a secret. Well, will you be outside the library window to-night at half-past eight?"

"Yes," promised William, "I'll be there."

Promptly on his arrival at the library window that evening it was opened cautiously by Clarinda.

"Are you there?" she whispered.

"Yes," hissed William.

"Well, look here. We're all going down to the barn for that dance in a minute, but—you'd better come in now and hide behind the curtain here. He's been glaring most horribly all through dinner, and we may need you before we go down. You slip in here. I'll come back as soon as I know when we're going."

William entered the room and took up his post behind the thick velvet curtains. After a short interval the door opened and two men entered. He peeped cautiously from his hiding-place. It was the benevolent-looking coin enthusiast and the young man who was his secretary. The secretary carried a small case.

"Got the key?" said the elder man, and his voice was no longer mellow and benevolent. It was curt and urgent.

"Yeah," snapped the secretary and took a key from his pocket. Together they opened a safe in the wall, took out several trays of coins, and, picking out one here and one there, put them into the small case. The collector then slipped the case into his pocket.

"I'll keep it on me," he snapped. "Safer."

"Let's clear off now," said the other as he closed the case and pocketed the key.

"Don't be a darned fool," replied Benevolence. "I'm going down to the barn with the others and in half an hour you can come in and tell me I've had an important telephone message from town. Then we'll get off at once. . . ."

"Right."

They went out. William had been too much occupied by fear of discovery to listen to this conversation. The men had been in, taken some coins from a safe, and gone out without finding him. That was all the incident meant to William—alas for his frequent dreams to catching criminals red-handed!

After a few minutes Clarinda reappeared.

"Nothing's happened yet," she whispered. "We're going down to the barn now. I think you ought to come too. I believe there's a loft."

"Yes, there's a loft all right," said William, who knew all about the barns for miles around, "an' there's a ladder up to it outside."

Well, I think you ought to be there," said Clarinda. "I have a sort of feeling that things are going to come to a head to-night. I must go now. . . . You *will* be there, won't you?"

"Yes," said William, "I'll be there all right."

After all, he reasoned, he could easily escape from the loft by the outside ladder if things came to too much of a head. . . .

He slipped through the kitchen garden to the barn and climbed the ladder to the loft. There he withdrew the trap-door and gazed down at the long decorated room. The house party was assembling. Robert and Clarinda, deeply engaged in confidential conversation, stood just beneath the trap-door. Theo approached them. Ignoring Robert, he fixed his eyes on Clarinda.

"May I have the second dance with you?" he said.

Clarinda's blue eyes flicked him up and down contemptuously.

"I'm afraid I'm engaged for all the dances this evening."

"To this chap?" sneered Theo, baring his teeth in the approved fashion of the villain through the ages.

"That's no concern of yours," said Clarinda icily, turning away from him.

Theo, too, turned away, deliberately jostling Robert as he did so.

"Look where you're going, can't you?" said Robert angrily.

For answer Theo jostled him again. Robert hit out. Theo hit back. Clarinda screamed. All was tumult and confusion. The guests separated the two fighting men and held them apart. Clarinda stepped into the middle with flashing eyes.

"It's time the truth were known," she said dramatically. She turned imperiously to Robert.

"Let me speak, Prince . . . "

Robert blinked at her in bewilderment. She pointed an accusing finger at Theo. "That man's name is not Theodore Horner."

"Shut up," muttered Theo fiercely.

"Do you deny," went on Clarinda, "that you are going under an assumed name?"

"No, I don't," shouted Theo, "but I don't see what business it is of yours."

"Well, I'll show you what business it is of mine," said Clarinda. She pointed to Robert and, turning to the assembled company, announced: "This man is a Russian prince."

Robert gaped at her.

"No, I'm not," he said.

"Oh, I *know* I promised to keep it secret," she said, "but don't you see—they must know—now that he's attempted your life."

"He hasn't attempted my life," said the literal Robert. "He's only given me a sock in the jaw."

"He's a Russian prince," went on Clarinda, again pointing to Robert. "He escaped from the revolution as a child with his family jewels, and this man"—she pointed now to Theo—"is a Bolshevist who has pursued him ruthlessly from his cradle."

"That's a lie," said Theo.

"DO YOU DENY THAT YOU ARE GOING UNDER AN ASSUMED
NAME?" DEMANDED CLARINDA.

"You've just admitted that you're going under an assumed name."

"Yes, but that's not the same as being a Bolshevist and pursuing people from their cradles."

"NO, I DON'T," SHOUTED THEO, "BUT WHAT BUSINESS IS IT OF YOURS?"

Sir Gerald suddenly stepped forward to take charge of the situation.

"What's your real name?" he said to Theo.

Theo hung his head in shame.

"Theodosius."

"Horner?"

"Yes."

Sir Gerald turned to Robert.

"And are you a Russian prince?" he said.

"No," replied Robert.

"Why did you tell her you were?"

"I didn't."

"Who did, then?"

It was at this moment that William, already leaning dangerously far out of his trap-door, engrossed by the dramatic scene beneath him, was startled by a rat running over his legs, overbalanced, and fell down upon the assembled company. He picked himself up. Robert's face became a frozen mask of horror.

"He did," said Clarinda, pointing to William. "He's a detective in constant communication with Scotland Yard and he's told to guard the prince."

Sir Gerald took firm hold of William's ear.

"Who gave you permission to come here?" he said grimly.

William remembered the permission that he had treasured against this occasion.

"*He* said I could," he answered triumphantly, glancing round the circle of guests for the white-bearded man. "*He* said I could come whenever I liked. I can't see him now, but he was in the library a minute ago putting coins out of the safe into his pocket."

Almost immediately the benevolent-looking old gentleman, abandoning his air of old age and benevolence, leapt from behind the circle of guests to the open door. Sir Gerald made a grab at him as he passed, but he escaped, leaving the patriarchal beard in Sir Gerald's hands. Theo pursued him, and flung himself upon him. He received a blow in the eye that sent him running back to the others for safety. Robert joined the pursuit, outstripped the others, seized the thief, received a blow that sent him staggering, sprang to his feet, received another that almost blinded him, continued the pursuit, caught the thief once more, was thrown off and kicked, continued the pursuit, and managed at last to hold him till the others came up.

\* \* \*

It was later in the evening. The dance was in full swing. Robert, black-eyed and bandaged, was sitting out with Clarinda.

"I can't tell you how sorry I am about the whole thing," he was saying. "It's all that little devil's fault. I'd no idea——"

"Well," said Clarinda thoughtfully, "just at first I was sorry to find you weren't a prince, but, when one comes to think of it, it would have been a very difficult life for us both. I mean, surrounded by enemies on every side and that sort of thing. No, I'm glad really that things have turned out as they have. . . . "

She was silent, gazing dreamily in front of her. It was quite film-like after all. A different type of film from the other, but quite definitely film-like.

"You see, it showed me how *brave* you are. I shall never forget the sight of you tackling that villain while Theodosius"—her lovely lip curled scornfully—"just moaned and asked for raw beef. Just as if anyone was *likely* to be carrying raw beef about at a dance." She saw a large and impressive "close up" of her face as she went on soulfully: "You may not be *a* prince, Robert, but you're *my* prince."

"*Angel!*" responded Robert satisfactorily.

# Chapter 8

# William Clears the Slums

The lady who came to the village to appeal for money for her pet slum-clearance scheme was, unfortunately, extremely pretty. Unfortunately, as far as William was concerned, that is, for, had this particular speaker not had this particular combination of dark hair and blue eyes, the probability is that William would have sat through the lecture without having the faintest idea even at the end what it was all about. William had long ago brought to perfection the art of sitting through lectures without having the faintest idea even at the end what they were all about. Expensive lecturers visited his school at regular intervals to interest the young idea in such things as the Political Situation (from a strictly non-party angle), the Manufacture of Soap (or biscuits or cloth or blotting-paper or aeroplanes), the Habits of Birds, the Wonders of the Deep, Wild Flower Collecting and kindred subjects, to all of which William could turn an ear carefully trained to complete deafness. He regarded these periodic lectures as oases in the desert of lessons, to be used for quiet meditation on his future plans, or unobtrusive games with his neighbours.

But this lecturer was not a school lecturer. She had come to address the Village Women's Guild on the Housing Problem, and the Vicar's wife had persuaded her to stay the night and address the Children's Guild the next day.

"It's so important," said the Vicar's wife earnestly, "to train them to have a social conscience."

A social conscience was one of the Vicar's wife's many hobby-horses, and it was with the idea of fostering it from earliest infancy that she had formed the Children's Guild. It had a large membership among the children of the neighbourhood. The Vicar's wife was a determined woman—her determination, in fact, bordered on ruthlessness—and by dint of ceaseless visits and an unfailing flow of eloquence she had persuaded most of the local mothers to enrol their children's names in the guild. As Mrs. Brown said to her husband:

"Yes, dear, I know it's ridiculous—I quite agree with you—but I feel I'd rather make William join anything on earth than have her coming here again talking about it. She's been five times this week already."

William's attitude, however, after a few meetings, had become so mutinous that this month Mrs. Brown herself accompanied him to the door of the Village Hall lest his absence from the meeting should inflict upon her another visit from the Vicar's wife.

He entered the room wearing his most ferocious scowl. Then his eye fell upon the lecturer, and the scowl cleared. He declined the invitation at the back bench to join them in a game of unofficial football and made his way to the front row, where he sat in the middle seat, his eyes fixed intently upon the lecturer's face. She was even prettier close to than she had been from the door. . . . She began to talk about too many people living together in one house so that they hadn't enough air to breathe, and how everyone ought to give money to get them out into bigger houses. It wasn't very interesting, so William began to imagine her imprisoned by Red Indians and himself fighting his way, single-handed, through several hundred of them to rescue her. Then he imagined her being captured by pirates and himself leaping from an aeroplane on to the pirate ship, forcing all the pirates to walk the plank—again single-handed—and sailing triumphantly home with her. He imagined her in several other similar situations, and by the time he had finished her lecture was over, and she was exhorting her audience to help in the good work by every means in their power, particularly by each bringing sixpence to her on the following day.

"I shall be at the Vicarage to-morrow, boys, and I want each of you to bring me sixpence there. I want you all to feel you're really helping. I'm sure that if you haven't got it you can earn it between now and then by doing some little service for some member of your families. I shall be *so* grateful for the sixpences you bring me," and she fluttered the blue eyes on whose help she evidently relied not a little in her task.

William walked home slowly and thoughtfully. He did not possess a sixpence and saw no immediate prospect of possessing one. His pocket-money was being indefinitely appropriated by his mother to pay for a new school cap. The old one—though only a month old—had been rendered unfit for wear by his habit of using it not only as a missile but also as a receptacle for water-weeds, water-creatures, stone, earth, clay and putty.

"It isn't fit to be seen," Mrs. Brown had said with unusual firmness, "and you must buy the new one yourself. I'm tired of paying for a new cap every other month. I don't know what you do with them."

William replied with spirit that he only did the same sort of things with them that everyone else did with them. What was a cap for, he demanded, if not to carry things about in? It was silly just wearing it on your head.

No one just wore a cap on their head. It had prob'ly got a bit wet with the water stuff and because he'd been damming a stream with it, but it was *his* cap and if he didn't mind wearing it he didn't see what business it was of anyone else's. But his eloquence expended itself in vain against Mrs. Brown's firmness. He must have a new cap, and he must have no pocket-money till it was paid for. William, switching from moral indignation to pathos, expressed a hope that if he died before the new cap was paid for she would not let the matter weigh too heavily on her conscience. Mrs. Brown reassured him on that point, but his bitterness deepened when he heard how much a new cap would cost.

"Crumbs!" he ejaculated in horror. "That means I'll be payin' for it till I'm an old man. Till I'm dead prob'ly. I never heard of anythin' costin' so much money as that. They're only bits of stuff cut round. I bet I could make one myself. I say," as a fresh idea struck him, "you jus' give me a bit of stuff an' I'll make one."

She refused, and William, recognising a certain tone in her voice as one upon which his utmost powers of eloquence would be wasted, resigned himself to the inevitable.

Now he surveyed his pocket-moneyless future gloomily. He longed to return to the blue-eyed lecturer to-morrow and lay a handsome contribution at her dainty feet, receiving in exchange the smile that had such a strangely exhilarating effect upon its recipient. Still— William was not a boy who wasted time in useless regret. He hadn't any money. He must set to work to earn some. He approached his sister Ethel first.

"Ethel," he said bluntly, "will you pay me sixpence if I do something for you?"

"Do what for me?" demanded Ethel.

"Anything," replied William. "I'll help you any way

you like if you'll pay me sixpence."

"Thanks," said Ethel sarcastically. "I've been helped by you before. I'd pay you sixpence not to help me."

"ETHEL," SAID WILLIAM, "WILL YOU PAY ME SIXPENCE IF I DO
SOMETHING FOR YOU?"

William hopefully accepted this offer, only to find to his disgust that it was immediately withdrawn.

He next set off to visit the only aunt who lived within walking-distance of his home. She was not a particularly generous aunt, but she had her weaker moments. He found her busy in her garden.

"I've come to see if I can help you," he announced, assuming what was meant to be an ingratiating smile.

"How kind of you!" said the aunt, and added solicitously: "Have you got toothache, dear boy?"

"No," said William coldly, and repeated: "Can I help you?"

"Certainly you can, dear," said the aunt, handing him a gardening fork. "You can weed that border over there for me. I shall be most grateful to you if you'd do that."

"Will you give me sixpence for it?" demanded William.

The aunt looked at him sternly.

"Sixpence?" she repeated.

"Yes," said William unmoved. "Sixpence."

Sternness gave place to horror in the aunt's countenance.

"Do you mean to say, William," she demanded, "that you want to be *paid* for doing a little thing like that for me?"

"Yes," said William simply.

"Of *course* I won't pay you, William," said the aunt distantly.

William carefully replaced his gardening fork in her basket.

"Good-bye," he said and set off again down the road.

His aunt's and Ethel's reception of his offers of help had discouraged him. He might walk the rest of the day, he considered gloomily, offering his services to people who didn't seem to know their value.

Suddenly he saw three little boys hanging over the gate of a small thatched cottage. It was one of those cottages in the village that were let generally to artists throughout the summer months. Last week it had been inhabited by a long-haired man with a beard and a short-haired woman in a smock. Evidently they had now gone, and new tenants had arrived.

"Hello," said the biggest boy.

He was about eight—an age that William generally treated with contempt, but this boy had freckles and a jolly impudent grin.

William stopped.

"Hello," he said. "What's your name?"

"Terry," answered the boy, and turning to the two younger ones, continued: "And these are the twins. They're called Billy and Dickie."

Billy and Dickie grinned through the bars of the gate.

"Hello," they said.

"What's your name?" said Terry.

"William Brown."

"Do you live near here?"

"Yes."

There was a long silence. Then William said:

"Can you do hand-springs?"

"No," said Terry, "but we've often tried, haven't we?"

"Yes," agreed the twins earnestly, "we jolly well have."

"Can you?" said Terry.

William proceeded shamelessly to show off. He did hand-springs. He walked on his hands across the road and back. He put one finger into each corner of his mouth and emitted a blood-curdling whistle. He vaulted the gate that led from the road into the field opposite. He turned a succession of swift somersaults for twenty yards or so down the road. When he had finished, he was dusty and tumbled, his collar and tie had wandered round to the back of his neck, his new cap reposed in the ditch. But the three pairs of eyes at the gate gazed at him with a reverence that bordered on idolatry.

"I *say*!" gasped Terry, gazing at him, "I say, could you teach us?"

William gazed at them judicially.

"*They're* too young," he said, indicating the twins, "but p'raps I might teach you. Come on an' try."

Terry came on and tried. He was thin and supple and proved an unexpectedly apt pupil. He didn't mind how dusty his hair or his suit became or whether his tie was at the front or the side or the back. He was, in fact, a boy after William's own heart.

"That's *jolly* good," said William at last. "You'll soon learn to do 'em all with a bit of practice."

"Thanks," said Terry gratefully, and added: "What sort of games do you play?"

"Oh, lots," said William. "I play Red Indians for one thing."

"I say, may we play Red Indians with you some time?" said Terry, breathless with eagerness.

"You can play now," replied William, who was tired of the insolvable problem of the slum-clearance contribution and wanted to forget it for a few hours. "You can come to the wood with me now if you like an' have a game."

"Can we come too?" squeaked the twins.

"Yes," said William graciously. "All of you come."

He led the little band to the wood, where the wigwam he had built the day before was still standing. He taught them how to make a fire and cook blackberries. He appointed one twin to be the squaw, and with the other and Terry he scouted the woods for enemies, killing wild beasts for food at frequent intervals. Finally Terry became so expert that he could take the character of chief of a hostile tribe, and he and William "scouted" each other through the thick undergrowth of brambles. At last the church clock could be heard striking six.

Terry rose reluctantly from his cover, showing a glowing if somewhat scratched face.

"I say, we'd better go now," he said. "It's bedtime. Thanks most awfully for letting us play with you. It's been *super*." ·

"That's all right," said William. "You played it jolly well. I'll come home with you."

They walked through the wood, arranging future meetings.

"You *will* let us play with you again, won't you?" said Terry anxiously.

"'Course," said William. "We'll have another game to-morrow."

He had been glad to forget his problem for a few hours, but now his thoughts were reluctantly turning to it again.

"Did you know," he said to Terry, "that some people live all squashed up in tiny houses an' that we've gotter gettem out?"

"The one we're in's like that," said Terry. "There's only two bedrooms, an' one's so small that it's just like a cupboard. Mother sleeps in that, an' me an' the twins in the other."

William looked at him sternly. "It's a slum then," he said, "an' you ought to be got out."

"Ought we?" said Terry placidly.

William was silent for a few minutes. He didn't possess sixpence and people wouldn't let him earn it. But at least he could do this. He could himself, alone and unaided, clear this slum that he had discovered. Surely, if he could tell the blue-eyed lecturer he had done that, she would be much more pleased than if he merely brought her sixpence.

"Look here," he said suddenly, "you come with me, an' I'll find you somewhere else to live. Where you've been living isn't big enough. You've gotter be got out."

"All right," said Terry trustingly.

He would have gone anywhere with, done anything for, this wonderful new friend who could do hand-springs, turn somersaults, emit ear-splitting whistles, and who had introduced him to the most fascinating game he had ever played in his life. "All right. Where'll we go? Look! There's Mother."

They had come in sight of the tiny thatched cottage again. A woman was standing at the gate, looking up and down the road, shading her eyes with her hand. She saw them and waved to them.

"Come on, children!" she called. "Bedtime!"

William realised the impossibility of putting his plan into action at this juncture, but it was far too fascinating to be abandoned altogether.

"Look here," he whispered urgently, "let her put you to bed, an' then, when she's gone downstairs, dress again an' come down to me. I'll be waiting for you in the field—behind the back garden. Don't tell her an' don't let her see you come down, 'cause she wouldn't under-stand. Then I'll find somewhere for you to go. You've gotter be got out."

"All right," said Terry happily, glad that this wonder-ful new game with this wonderful new friend was going to continue into the night.

"Can we come too?" squeaked the twins.

"Yes," said William. "All of you come. You've all gotter be got out."

"Come along, children!" the woman at the gate called again.

The three boys ran towards her, and William melted unobtrusively into the landscape.

In about half an hour the three boys joined him in the field behind the back garden. Their faces shone clean

from their bedtime baths, and their clothes bore
evidence of hasty dressing.

"We didn't bother with ties or garters or anything like
that," said Terry. "That's all right, isn't it? I say—
where are we going?"

A somewhat harassed frown replaced William's smile
of welcome.

His first plan of taking them home with him had been
dismissed upon mature reflection. Not only was it
fraught with danger, but it would merely transfer the
overcrowding from one house to another. His next plan
of housing his protégés in the old barn had been
dismissed on the same ground.

"Yes, where are we going?" squeaked the twins
eagerly, ready for any adventure into which this marvel-
lous being should lead them.

William raised his eyes in silent perplexity—and they
fell upon the chimneys of the Hall, which showed plainly
through its belt of trees.

The Hall was empty except for a caretaker. Violet
Elizabeth was away at school, and her parents were
spending the autumn abroad and in Scotland, and had
sent their servants home on board wages. The Hall
possessed more than twenty bedrooms—far more than
the Botts ever used, even when they were at home.
Here, then, at this door lay the solution of his problem.
The blue-eyed lecturer had said that people must
be taken from the small houses where they were all
crowded together and put in larger houses where there
was plenty of room for them. He would take his little
band from the thatched cottage to the Hall. There was
ample room for them in the Hall. Mrs. Bott was a
generous and sympathetic woman, despite her lack of
education, and William felt sure that she would wish to
aid in the good work of slum clearing on which he was

engaged. The caretaker was a different proposition altogether. She was one of William's oldest and most inveterate enemies, and William decided not to risk the failure of his scheme by consulting her about it. He decided to take Mrs. Bott's permission for granted and install his protégés in the Hall as quickly and secretly as possible. . . .

"Come on with me," he said. "I'm going to take you to a jolly nice place."

Trustingly they accompanied him across the fields to the Hall and gleefully allowed themselves to be concealed in a shrubbery while he went to reconnoitre. He made his way round to the kitchen window and peeped in cautiously. Fate was evidently on his side. Instead of the caretaker there dozed by the kitchen fire an old woman whom William recognised as the caretaker's aunt, who came to take her place when the caretaker herself had gone to see her mother. The caretaker's aunt was wholly deaf and partially blind. William's spirits rose. Things weren't going to be as difficult as he had thought they might be. He next crept round in search of an open window and soon discovered the pantry window conveniently open at the top. He entered, and tiptoed past the open door of the kitchen, where deep rhythmic sounds assured him that he had little to fear as yet from the caretaker's aunt. He slipped up the back stairs to the first floor and began to explore the bedrooms. There were quite a lot of them, and they were all lofty and spacious enough to satisfy the most determined and particular of slum clearers, but they were rather too near the operations of the caretaker to be quite safe for William's purpose.

He found a small spiral staircase leading to the top floor, and there he discovered the servants' bedrooms, dismantled and secure from discovery. He chose the

three largest and set about preparing them for his
rescued slum dwellers. There were no bedclothes on the
beds, but there was a large cupboard on the landing, full
of bedclothes of every description, and William, staggering into each room with armfuls of blankets, had soon
prepared the beds in a rough and ready fashion for their
occupants.

He then went down to summon them and found them
still crouching in the shrubbery in a state of gleeful
anticipation.

"Come on," he said. "I've got you some jolly fine
bedrooms."

He pushed and pulled them through the pantry
window, led them on tiptoe past the kitchen door, up the
back stairs, up the spiral staircase to the three rooms.

"Now you can go to bed," he announced proudly.

They smiled at him eagerly.

"Have we come to stay with you?" demanded Terry.

"Y-yes," assented William. "In a sort of way you
have."

"That's ripping. And can we play with you all
to-morrow?"

"Yes," said William. "I'll come for you first thing in
the morning."

"I'm hungry!" said the twins simultaneously.

"All right," said William. "You jus' get into bed first,
an' then I'll go down an' find you something to eat."

Under William's directions they removed their suits
and got into bed in their underclothes.

"Now you stay here," said William, "an I'll go'n' find
you something to eat."

He slipped down the spiral staircase and was just
crossing the main landing on his way to the back
staircase when he heard voices in the hall. He stopped. It
was Mr. and Mrs. Bott. Aghast, he stepped into a

convenient linen cupboard and waited. Mrs. Bott's voice, raised shrilly in order to reach the deaf caretaker, floated up the stairs.

"NOW YOU CAN GO TO BED," ANNOUNCED WILLIAM PROUDLY. "I'M HUNGRY!" SAID THE TWINS SIMULTANEOUSLY.

"Yes, I know you didn't expect us. Mr. Bott's got a nasty cold and we've had a very bad crossing, and he didn't feel like going straight up to Scotland. He wanted to come home for a rest on the way. Yes, it's quite all right about Mrs. Miggs. I said she could go and see her mother whenever she liked. No, I know you've no supper for us. Just eggs and a cup of tea will do nicely, won't it, Botty? I think Mr. Bott will go to bed at once. His cold's very heavy in his head. Bring the eggs up to our bedroom. Come on, Botty love."

They ascended the stairs and entered their bedroom. Unfortunately the linen cupboard in which William had taken refuge was just opposite their bedroom door, and, as Mrs. Bott left this half open, he had no chance of escape.

"Now, Botty love, you'll feel better when you've got to bed and had a nice cup of tea."

"No, I shan't," replied Mr. Bott's usually cheerful voice, now sunk deep in gloom. "I shall never feel better no more. I've come 'ome to die, that's what I 'ave."

"Nonsense, love," said his wife briskly. "You always feel like that when you've just had a bad crossing. And, of course, what with the cold in your head an' all it's just a bit worse than usual, that's all."

"I'm dyin', that's what I am," repeated Mr. Bott lugubriously.

"Go on, Botty! People don't die of colds in their heads. Nor yet of crossings. You'll feel as different as different when you've had a nice rest."

Soon the caretaker's aunt brought up a tray with tea and eggs, but the door was still left half open, and William dared not emerge from his hiding-place. He considered the possibility of stepping out boldly and explaining to Mrs. Bott the work of mercy that he had undertaken on her behalf. But his courage failed him. It was one thing to take Mrs. Bott's permission for granted in her absence. It was quite another to confront her with the present situation. No, all he could do now was to watch and listen and hope for the best. The complete silence that reigned on the servants' floor encouraged him to hope that his charges had gone to sleep. There came the clinking of china and teaspoons from Mr. and

Mrs. Bott's bedroom and the sound of intermittent conversation. The note of gloom was gradually vanishing from Mr. Bott's voice.

"Yes, love," he admitted at last, "I really do feel a little better."

"'*Course* you do," said his wife briskly. "I shouldn't be surprised if you're well enough to go on to Scotland first thing to-morrow morning."

"Well, I may be, if I go on like this," he admitted guardedly.

"'Course you will," said his wife again. "You go to bed directly we've had this an' get a good night's rest an' you'll feel as perky as perky to-morrow."

"Not perky," said Mr. Bott in a rather shocked tone. "I don't think I shall ever feel perky again. But—yes, I certainly am better. Yes, I'll have another cup of tea and the other egg, if you're sure you don't want it."

"Do you know what they told me at the post office, Botty, when I called about the letters on our way up here?"

"No, love. We might have some more bread and butter, don't you think? I'm feeling quite hungry now. Not perky, mind you," he went on rather reprovingly as if the unsuitability of the word still rankled, "only hungry."

"Of course, dearie," said Mrs. Bott. "I'll go down for some more bread and butter in a minute. It's no use ringing. She won't hear. What was I saying? Oh, they told me at the post office that Lady Walton's staying here. At Rose Cottage. You know Lady Walton. You see her photo in the *Tatler* and suchlike. They've got a house in London and a place in Surrey—both of them as big as palaces. And they say the thing she likes to do best of all is to take a small cottage in the country with her children without even a servant, and do the cooking an' all herself. She's come here while her husband's in Scotland shooting. You've heard of her, haven't you, Botty?"

"Can't say I have," said Mr. Bott rather sulkily. He did not share his wife's passionate interest in high life, and he considered that it was rather soon after his recovery for the conversation to leave his symptoms.

"Oh, Botty! She's one of the most famous society hostesses. Her house parties down in Surrey are the great social events of the year. I've often read so in the *Tatler* and suchlike. Oh, Botty, if only I could go to a place like that I'd die happy."

"*You* needn't worry about dyin'," said Mr. Bott morosely. "D'you know I've used nine handkerchiefs to-day?"

"Oh, but, Botty, you feel better."

"Y-yes, I know I do. But not perky."

"I'll go and get the bread and butter."

She came to the bedroom door then stopped.

From the floor above came the short sharp cry that a child makes when it half awakes from an uneasy sleep.

"Good heavens!" she said. "Whatever's that?"

"I didn't hear anything," said her husband. "Tell her plenty of butter on, love. And if there's anything else in the larder you might bring it up. I'm feeling a lot better. Not perky—but a lot better."

"But didn't you hear that noise, Botty?"

"No. There wasn't any noise. It was your imagination."

"It wasn't my imagination, Botty. There's someone up there."

"Well, if there is, it's painters or someone like that that Mrs. Miggs has got in."

"Painters don't make that noise."

"Painters make any sort of a noise."

There was a silence, during which Mrs. Bott evidently braced up her courage.

"I'm going up to see what it was, Botty," she said at last in a tone of grim determination. "I'm going up now and nothing shall stop me."

"You'll find it was only your imagination," said Mr. Bott, "and when you come down you won't forget about the bread and butter, will you?"

Mrs. Bott armed herself with a poker in one hand and a coal-shovel in the other, and set off for the servants' floor.

A few moments later she returned, and William could see through the crack in his cupboard door that she was very pale.

"Botty," she said in a faint voice, "there's three children asleep in bed up there."

"There couldn't possibly be," said Mr. Bott firmly. "I told you it was all your imagination."

"You can't imagine three children asleep in bed," protested Mrs. Bott.

"I don't see why you shouldn't imagine that as well as anything else," contradicted Mr. Bott.

"But they're *real,* I tell you," said Mrs. Bott wildly. "I tell you they're *real.* Who can they be?"

"Wake 'em up an' ask 'em," suggested Mr. Bott.

"I *couldn't,* Botty. They're so sound asleep it would be *cruel* to wake them. Besides, they'd only start crying or something. I'm going down to ask Mrs. Miggs's aunt about them."

"Well, don't forget to bring up the bread and butter," Mr. Bott reminded her.

After a few moments she returned, breathless and harassed.

"She says she knows nothing about them, Botty. She'll hardly believe they're there."

"I'm not sure that I do," growled Mr. Bott. "You're always imagining burglars an' suchlike."

"Three children in bed's different from burglars," returned Mrs. Bott with spirit. "Anyone can imagine burglars, but I've never heard of anyone imagining three children in bed."

"Neither did I till you started," said her husband. "Did you remember the bread and butter?"

"No, I didn't. I'll go down again in a minute. . . . Look here, Botty, I believe I know what it is. I believe Mrs. Miggs is having her sister's little boys here for a holiday while we're away. No reason why she shouldn't, of course, though I do think she might have asked, don't you?" Perplexity clouded her brow again. "But she's been away all day. Who put them to bed? And, if that was it, Mrs. Miggs's aunt would know about them."

"If you're going down to ask her again," her husband suggested patiently, "you'll remember the bread and butter, won't you?"

"Yes, I'll go now."

She went to the bedroom door. Immediately the telephone bell began to ring violently in the hall below.

"I wonder who that can be," said Mrs. Bott. "I'll answer it. Mrs. Miggs's aunt won't hear a word."

William heard her voice down in the hall, growing more and more excited, then she came upstairs again almost running.

"Oh, Botty," she gasped, "it's that Lady Walton I was telling you about that's staying at Rose Cottage! She's just rung up. She said that her brother and his family are coming over to England on leave from India next year, and she's looking for a place for them to spend the summer, and she's just heard in the village that we want to let the Hall next summer while we're abroad, so she's rung up to see if she can come and look over it now.

Oh, *Botty,* isn't it *thrilling!*"

"You didn't remember the bread and butter while you were down, did you?" said Mr. Bott.

"No, I didn't, love, but I'll go down again now."

"My stomach's beginning to feel quite empty again," said Mr. Bott pathetically.

By the time she had returned with the bread and butter the front door bell announced the arrival of the visitor.

"Oh, Botty, I'm *that* excited," said Mrs. Bott. "Think what it would mean to us to have a person like that taking the house! Oh, dear, what's my hair like, love? Do I look all right?"

She flew downstairs, and William heard her excited voice, punctuated at intervals by the visitor's deep drawl, as they made the tour of the house.

William would have liked to seize the opportunity to escape, but the bedroom door was still open, and Mr. Bott, sitting over the fire in his dressing-gown, eating bread and butter and drinking tea, was in full view of the cupboard door that concealed him.

He peered anxiously through the crack of the cupboard as Mrs. Bott and her visitor passed along the landing. And there he got his first shock. For the lady to whom Mrs. Bott was showing her house was the lady whom William had seen leaning over the gate of the thatched cottage calling her children in to bed—those children who now slumbered peacefully on the top floor of the house she was inspecting.

"I think it's all perfectly charming," she was saying. "Just what my brother wants. I'll write to him at once."

She walked to the foot of the spiral staircase and looked up. "Where does this lead?"

Suddenly all the smiling vivacity left Mrs. Bott's countenance. In the excitement of showing her titled visitor round her home, she had forgotten the mysterious children on the servants' floor. It would be dreadful to have to confess that she didn't know who they were or where they'd come from.

"T-that only leads to the servants' rooms," she stammered. "It's not worth going up to them. Really, Lady Walton, it isn't."

But Lady Walton's curiosity was aroused.

"I think I'd like to see them," she said. "I know my sister-in-law will want particulars of the whole house."

The colour stood out in blotches on Mrs. Bott's face. Her embarrassment was painful. What *would* she think of her, having three children up there and knowing nothing about them?

"No, reelly it's not worth going up there, Lady Walton. Reelly it's not. It's—it's—it's the stairs I'm thinking of. They're dangerous."

"They look perfectly safe. I suppose the servants use them?"

"Yes, what I meant was you'll find them so tiring. They're *dreadfully* tiring stairs. Reelly they are. . . . Oh, look, Lady Walton, I never showed you this little dressing-room, did I?"

They turned aside into the dressing-room. Mr. Bott himself had closed the bedroom door. The coast was clear. Like a streak William slipped from the cupboard and vanished up the spiral staircase. Somehow he must get the trio out of the way before their mother found them. But it was too late. Hardly had he reached the top step when Lady Walton set foot on the bottom one. She had merely thrown a glance round the dressing-room and had immediately returned to the mysterious staircase. Mrs. Bott's manner had aroused her suspicions. Something queer was going on up there, and she was determined to find out what it was. Mrs. Bott panted after her up the staircase. After all, she was thinking, she needn't have got so fussed up. She needn't say she didn't know who the children were. She'd say that they were her housekeeper's sister's children, who were spending their holidays there. And, of course, they really might be, for all she knew, though it wasn't like Mrs. Miggs not to have asked her.

William had just had time to fling himself into Terry's room and under the bed when they appeared on the landing.

They first entered the room where Dickie lay asleep. Mrs. Bott drew a deep breath.

"This is my caretaker's sister's child," she said. "Her three little boys are spending their holidays here."

Lady Walton looked down at all that could be seen of her son—a bright tousled head and the curve of one rosy cheek. How ridiculously like Dickie, she thought. Really, if she hadn't put Dickie to bed with her own hands only an hour ago, she wouldn't have believed it wasn't Dickie.

"He's very like one of my own little boys," she said.

"Is he?" said Mrs. Bott. "They're nice rooms, aren't they? Well, there's no need to go through all of them, is there? They're all just like this."

"I'd like to see them, please," said Lady Walton firmly.

They entered the next room, where the other twin lay asleep. He, too, lay with his face buried in the pillow so that little of his face could be seen, but that little was so amazingly like Billy that Lady Walton gave a sudden gasp.

"Is this another of your caretaker's sister's children?" she said.

"Yes," replied Mrs. Bott.

"Twins, I suppose?"

"Er—yes," said Mrs. Bott, and went on hastily: "Well, we needn't go into the next room, because it's just like this, and——"

"I'd like to see it, please," said Lady Walton again.

Mrs. Bott opened the door, and they both entered. Lady Walton gazed down at Terry, who also lay with his freckled face buried into the bedclothes. It might, of course, be possible that this woman's caretaker's sister had three little boys bearing a miraculous likeness to Terry and the twins. But the coincidence could not extend to the scratches that ran across Terry's smooth freckled cheeks. Only an hour ago she had stroked those scratches tenderly and said: "Darling, where *have* you been to get all scratched like this?" and he had replied: "Playing Red Indians."

Suddenly Terry opened his eyes, smiled at her, murmured: "Hello, Mummy," then turned over and went to sleep again.

Lady Walton's mind worked quickly. She saw at once what had happened. From the beginning she had thought there was something strange in the shuttered servantless state of the house, for which the woman had given some lame excuse about having come home unexpectedly because her husband had a cold in his head. It was indeed a curious Fate that had led her straight into the den of the gang that had kidnapped her own children. They were, of course, obvious game for the kidnapper, now she came to think of it. Her husband was a prominent member of the Cabinet, her father was a world-famous millionaire. These people must have laid their plans months back, as soon as she took the cottage. They'd probably taken this house for the purpose. What they hadn't reckoned with was her arriving to look over the house like this. No wonder the woman had tried to prevent her coming upstairs.

She turned to Mrs. Bott, whose eyes were almost starting out of her head with horror and bewilderment.

"Mrs. Bott, or whatever your real name is," she said slowly and distinctly, "why did you tell me that these children are your caretaker's sister's? You're perfectly aware that they're my children."

Terror and amazement deprived Mrs. Bott of the power of speech. She opened and shut her mouth in silence like an expiring fish.

"I'm not going to appeal to your compassion or your honour," went on Lady Walton calmly, "because a woman—or rather a thing in the shape of a woman—who can stoop to the dastardly crime of kidnapping children can't know the meaning of either. But I tell you what I'm going to do. I'm going to tie you up and lock you in this room—I'm a good deal stronger than I look, and I'm in very good condition—then I'm going to dress my children and take them away. And I warn you that the first thing I do when I get out of this house will be to communicate with Scotland Yard, and I'll never rest, and my husband will never rest, till we've brought you and your whole gang to justice. If you try to rouse your gang now I warn you that it will be the worse for you. . . . "

"No!" screamed Mrs. Bott wildly. "No, no, *no*! I didn't do it. I swear I didn't do it."

Then she sat down on the nearest chair and went into hysterics.

Lady Walton caught a movement under the bed. She bent down and drew out William.

"Another of your victims," she said sternly to the sobbing Mrs. Bott. "How many more children have you got imprisoned up here, you heartless wretch?"

She laid her hand tenderly upon William's head. "Where did she take you from, my poor child?"

Terry, roused again by Mrs. Bott's hysterics, sat up in bed and smiled at William.

"WHERE DID SHE TAKE YOU FROM, MY POOR CHILD?" LADY
WALTON ASKED WILLIAM.

"He's William," he said to his mother. "He's the boy that brought us here."

Lady Walton turned to her hostess.

"Your child, then, I suppose?" she said coldly.

"No, *no!*" screamed Mrs. Bott between her sobs.

"Why did you bring them here?" said Lady Walton to William. "Did this woman force you to?"

"No," admitted William. "No, she didn't exactly force me to."

"I DIDN'T KNOW ANYTHING ABOUT THEM," SOBBED MRS. BOTT.

"Why did you bring them then?"

William drew a deep breath. The moment of explanation had arrived. It could no longer be evaded or postponed.

"Well," he began slowly, "really it wasn't anything to do with her. I'll tell you all about it if you'll listen." Mrs. Bott ceased her hysterics to listen. "You see, I brought them here 'cause I was slum clearing."

"You were *what*?" said Lady Walton.

"Slum clearing," he repeated distinctly. "I was clearing out the slums an' I jus' happened to start with them, that was all."

Bit by bit the story came out. As it came out the grimness in Lady Walton's eye was replaced by a twinkle. Mrs. Bott's hysterics ebbed and flowed spasmodically.

"I didn't know anything about them," she assured Lady Walton sobbingly. "I didn't know where they'd come from nor nothing; an' I didn't like to wake them, an' then when you came I didn't like to tell you I didn't know where they'd come from, an'—oh dear," she turned reproachfully to William, "it's all this *wicked* boy's fault."

Lady Walton sat down on Terry's bed and laughed.

"When I think of the names I called you," she said to Mrs. Bott, "will you *ever* forgive me?"

Before Mrs. Bott could reply, Billy woke up in the next room and, finding himself in strange surroundings, began to cry. His crying woke Dickie, who began to cry too. Lady Walton and Mrs. Bott went in to comfort and dress them. William followed, making voluble excuses for his conduct.

"Well, how was I to *know*?" he demanded. "They said they were all squashed up in a little house an' *she* said people like that had better be got out."

At last the three children were dressed and ready to accompany their mother back to the cottage. Lady Walton gave way at intervals to helpless laughter.

"I've never come across anything so funny," she said. "My husband will never stop teasing me about it. And you're going on to Scotland to-morrow, Mrs. Bott?"

"Yes," said Mrs. Bott. "My husband's feeling much better."

"But we must meet again to have a good laugh over this," went on Lady Walton. "We're giving a small house party at our place in Surrey next month. I wonder if you'd care to join it?"

A seraphic smile lit up Mrs. Bott's countenance.

"Oh, I'd *love* to," she said. "I can't tell you how I'd love to."

"Good! I'll send you all details when I get back to town. The second week probably. And now I must get these sleepy little people home to bed."

Mrs. Bott went down to see her off at the front door. Turning away from it, she ran into William, who was trying to slip away unobtrusively behind them.

"Now, William," she said, "I hope you're thoroughly ashamed of yourself."

She tried to speak sternly, but the seraphic smile still lingered on her face. A house party at Lady Walton's. Perhaps she'd even see herself in one of those groups in the *Tatler*. Well, after this she'd be *somebody* for the rest of her life. . . .

"How was I to *know*?" demanded William for the hundredth time.

Mrs. Bott looked at him. Now she came to think of it, she owed it to William. If it hadn't been for William she'd never have been invited to Lady Walton's house party. She took a shilling from her purse and slipped it into his hand.

"You don't deserve it, William, after the dreadful way you've behaved, but——"

"Oh, *thanks*," gasped William.

\*　　\*　　\*

He walked jauntily down to the village clutching his shilling firmly in his hand. He'd decided not to give it to the slum-clearance fund after all. He was a good deal less in sympathy with the aims of that fund than he had been a few hours before. Moreover, the memory of the blue blue eyes of the lecturer was slowly fading. He remembered having seen a water-pistol of a specially superior kind—marked 1/-—in the window of the village shop. He had gazed at it wistfully as one gazes at the unattainable. But it wasn't unattainable any longer. He set off briskly in the direction of the village shop.

# Chapter 9

# The Outlaws and
the Fifth

As November the Fifth approached, the thoughts of the
Outlaws and their gang turned instinctively to fireworks
and bonfires.

Usually the financial aspect of the situation was its
weakest point, but this year Ginger had received an
unexpected tip of ten shillings from his grandmother,
and so the Outlaws could stand with their noses glued as
usual to the windows of such shops as included fireworks
in their display, but without the usual feeling of
hopelessness at their hearts. They had ten shillings to
spend on fireworks, and the prospect seemed one of
unbounded magnificence.

As William said:

"We can jolly well get some of almost every kind of
firework there is for that, an' I bet we'll beat Hubert
Lane's show to cinders."

For the rivalry between the Outlaws' gang and Hubert
Lane's gang, far from having been extinguished by the
Vicar's wife's attempts at pacification, had been fanned
to even greater heat.

Usually Hubert Lane did not go in for fireworks,
considering them noisy and dangerous and an unnecessary waste of money, but, hearing that the Outlaws were
about to hold a firework exhibition on a large scale, he

decided to enter into competition.

He gathered his gang together and told them to canvass their relations for funds. The canvassing produced little result, but that did not matter, as Hubert himself possessed a mother of the fond variety, who gave her darling whatever he chose to ask for. When he asked her for a pound to spend on fireworks, she hesitated only because of the danger thus threatened to Hubert's precious person.

"But, darling," she said, "they're such horrid things. You might get hurt."

"Not me," Hubert reassured her. "I'll keep well out of the way, you bet. Old Bertie's going to let all the things off."

For Bertie Franks had long since tired of having a gang of his own and had rejoined his old chief, who was making him pay for his defection by detailing him off to do all the unpleasant work connected with the gang.

"Yes," he continued with a snigger, "I'll jolly well see that old Bertie lets 'em off. He can set 'em up, too, an' get everything ready. An' I'll jolly well make him buy some of them."

"Well, darling," cooed Mrs. Lane, "as long as you don't get hurt—that's all I care about."

"Oh, I won't get hurt," Hubert assured her. "You can bet your life I won't get hurt."

The news soon went round to the Outlaws that the Hubert Laneites had the magnificent sum of one pound to spend on fireworks, and that they were determined to make the Outlaws' firework display, as Hubert put it, "look like a burnt match". The Outlaws, stung by this remark, redoubled their efforts, peforming menial tasks for their families in return for halfpence, displaying fulsome politeness to moneyed relatives, offering their possessions for sale at less than their market value. The sum total of this vast expenditure of energy was half a crown.

"Half a crown!" said William bitterly. "After cleaning their shoes an' sweeping up their leaves an' openin' doors for them an' saying 'Please' and 'Thank you' till your face aches—half a crown!"

"We can't get better fireworks than Hubert Lane, anyway," said Ginger gloomily. "Even s'pose we got a pound like he's got, he'd only go off to his mother an' get another pound an' it'd be jus' the same."

"Tell you what," said William, struck by a sudden idea, "let's have a guy. He'll never think of a guy. An' anyway he can't buy a guy. He'd have to make one. An' he couldn't make one for nuts."

"What sort of a guy shall we have?" asked Douglas.

"Let's have someone everyone knows," said William thoughtfully, "so's we can make it look like him. Let's have——" He stopped to consider.

"Major Blake!" finished Henry excitedly.

"Major Blake!" they all cried out in delighted agreement.

Major Blake had rented the Hall from the Botts for the autumn, and carried on a fierce warfare against the Outlaws in their capacity of universal trespassers. When Mr. Bott was at the Hall they had trespassed freely in his park and grounds, and Mr. Bott had made no objection. Major Blake, however, objected strongly, and his objection took a practical form. He pursued the Outlaws whenever he saw them on his property, and, being unexpectedly nimble on his feet, generally caught at least two of them, to whom he would administer corporal punishment with the stout stick he always carried. The Outlaws regarded him with feelings of bitter hostility.

"Yes, let's have *him*!" said William joyfully. "It'll be

jolly fun seein' him burn, won't it? Him an' his rotten ole stick. Wish he could jolly well see it too."

The spirits of the Outlaws rose as they contemplated this spectacle.

"Bet ole Hubert won't have anything like that!" said Ginger.

"Well, be jolly careful not to let him find out we're having one," said William. "Don't go talking about it, an' try'n' look as if we'd never thought of it."

The Outlaws promised joyfully to do this, and the next day they set to work on the manufacture of the guy. They worked long and earnestly. Fortunately the gallant soldier was easy to caricature. He had a sanguine complexion, a large drooping moustache, bristling, upstanding eyebrows, and a monocle affixed to a broad black ribbon. The Outlaws bought an ordinary mask and with much care and labour transformed it into an unmistakable likeness of their enemy. A pot of rouge, purloined from Ethel's bedroom, heightened the already rosy colour of the cheeks; strands of wool from an old black rug were glued on to form the drooping moustache and the bristly eyebrows. Half of a pair of tinted spectacles that Ginger's mother had bought at Woolworth's during a heat-wave, attached to an old bootlace, formed the monocle. The costume was at first a difficulty, as the Major always wore brown suits of a striking check pattern, and, though Henry could have supplied a dark suit that his father had presented to his mother for her rummage-sale cupboard, it was felt that this would have completely destroyed the illusion.

It was Douglas who brought the glorious news that a scarecrow had appeared that day in the Hall kitchen garden dressed in one of the Major's cast-off brown check suits, even including the cap.

"We'll go'n' get it to-night," decided William

promptly. "We'll go as soon as it gets dark an' take it off it."

The expedition had all the elements of lawlessness and danger that the Outlaws loved. They crept in single file through the Hall shrubbery and into the Hall kitchen garden. It took a fairly long time to disrobe the scarecrow, and more than once they fled, leaving the work half done, thinking they heard footsteps. It was finished in safety at last, however, and they crept away through the darkness, the Major's suit bundled up under William's arm. A stout stick taken from the hedgerows completed the effect. Certainly, when a sack had been stuffed to represent the body, and two long sticks fixed on to it to represent the legs, it was an impressive caricature. When the coat and waistcoat had been put on over the sack, and the trousers drawn over the sticks, it was, the Outlaws decided, almost as much like Major Blake as he was like himself.

Competition between the two gangs still raged fast and furious. An aunt of Henry's had sent him down a box of fireworks from a London shop which considerably diminished the difference between the preparations of the two gangs. Hubert Lane, moreover, had discovered that the Outlaws were making a guy and had immediately set his followers at work upon a guy for his own bonfire. It was, reported the members of the Outlaws' gang who saw it through the windows of the Lanes' wood-house, an almost pitifully ordinary guy—a mask affixed to a sack, and wrapped in an old coat of Mrs. Lane's. However many more fireworks Hubert managed to acquire, however magnificent a bonfire he might make, his guy would be put completely to shame by the Outlaws' guy.

As the day approached the members of the two gangs began anxiously to watch the signs of the weather. A wet day would have ruined all their hopes. But the day dawned fine and cloudless, and they set to work early in the afternoon building up the structure of the bonfire and arranging their fireworks.

The two bonfires were to be held in the field behind the old barn, and the Outlaws' hearts sank as they saw the undeniable superiority of the Laneite's preparation. Then they rose again as they remembered their guy and imagined him sitting on high amid the blaze. There was no doubt that he would dominate the whole scene. No amount of extra fireworks would quite make up for him.

Having finished their preparations—all but the guy, which was to remain in the disused garage attached to Ginger's house till the last moment for safety—William went down to the village shop to see if any fireworks could be bought cheap at the last minute. At the door they met Hubert Lane, bent presumably on the same errand. They were both gathering breath for the exchange of insults that was the usual forerunner of hostilities, when a little girl walked out of the shop. She was a little girl whom they had never seen before—an attractive little girl with dimples and a mop of dark curls.

"Hello," she greeted them in friendly fashion.

Hastily they dropped their expressions of ferocity and assumed ingratiating smiles.

"Hello," they replied simultaneously.

"I've been to buy some sweets," she said. "Will you have one?"

She held out a paper bag.

They wiped their grimy hands down their trousers and each took an acid drop, still maintaining the ingratiating smiles.

"What are you going to buy?" went on the little girl.

"Fireworks," said William and Hubert simultaneously, exchanging suspicious glances.

The little girl gave a cry of delight.

"Oh, of *course.* It's Guy Fawkes' Day. I'd quite forgotten. Are you having fireworks? How lovely! May I come?"

"We're having different ones," said William, exchanging another hostile glance with Hubert. "We're having two bonfires an' two lots of fireworks. You see," he explained, "we belong to different gangs."

"How exciting!" said the little girl. "Whose is going to be the best?"

"Mine is," said Hubert promptly.

"Oh, is it?" said William meaningfully. "You jolly well wait and see."

"Who is going to judge them?" said the little girl.

"We don't want a judge," said Hubert. "There won't . be any doubt which is best."

"Oh, won't there?" said William again. "You jolly well wait and see."

"But you *must* have a judge," said the little girl. "You must have a judge, and you must have a prize for the best."

A gleam came into Hubert's eye at the word "prize".

"Who'll give a prize?" demanded Hubert.

The little girl thought for a moment, then gave a little skip of delight.

"I know!" she said. "I'll give a camera. I had one given me for my birthday last week, and I don't want it, because I've got two already. I'll give that. It's a good camera. It'll make a lovely prize."

The gleam deepened in Hubert's eye.

"I jus' wanted a camera," he said.

"Who said you were goin' to get it?" demanded William.

"Not much doubt I'll get it," sneered Hubert.

William tried to think of a better response than "Oh,

isn't there? You jolly well wait and see," but, not being able to, made it once more.

"Where did you say you were going to have the bonfires?" she said.

"Over there," replied William. "In the field where the old barn is."

"What time?"

"Seven o'clock."

The little girl was now so excited that she was dancing about on the tips of her toes.

"I'll be there, and I'll bring the prize and I'll judge them and . . . *I know!*" Her excitement was almost more than she could contain. "Let's have a feast in the old barn afterwards. I'll bring the feast, shall I?"

They stared at her, impressed and half incredulous.

"Will you *really*?" said William.

"'Course I will," she said. "You all come and meet me down the road at seven and help carry the things, will you?"

"*Rather!*" said William fervently.

"I must go and get ready quickly then," said the little girl.

She waved good-bye to them and danced off down the road out of sight. They stared after her, still dumbfounded. It was not till she had disappeared that it occurred to them that they had not asked her her name or where she lived.

"Bet she was pulling our legs," said Hubert.

"Bet she wasn't," said William indignantly.

"Doesn't matter to you whether she was or she wasn't, anyway," said Hubert, "'cause you won't get the prize."

"Oh, won't we?" said William, allowing his natural pugnacity full play now that the civilising influence of the little girl was withdrawn. "Jus' you jolly well say that again."

Hubert said it again and promptly took to his heels, pursued by William. William, however, did not pursue him far, being anxious to rejoin his gang and impart to them the momentous news of the little girl's offer.

"An' I'm jolly sure she meant it," he concluded earnestly. "She didn't look the sort of person that doesn't mean things. You can always tell."

"But who is she, anyway?" demanded Ginger.

William had to admit that he didn't know.

"I forgot to ask," he explained. "I've never seen her before, but I'm sure it's all right."

"It would be jolly nice to have a camera," said Henry.

"Yes, but shall we get it?" demanded Douglas gloomily. "They've got twice as many fireworks as what we have."

"Yes, but there's our guy," William reminded him. "I bet our guy'll get us the prize all right."

Certainly every time they went to look at the impressive caricature of Major Blake reposing in the garage their hearts thrilled with pride. They had never seen such a guy. No one, they were sure, had ever seen such a guy. It was a super super guy *de luxe*. They could not resist various further touches, such as a pipe in the mouth and a dab of red on the nose.

Towards seven o'clock the two gangs brought out their fireworks and placed them in readiness. Then they brought out their guys, shrouded in sacking, and placed them on the bonfire piles. Though nothing could so far be seen of either, the Outlaws thrilled with the knowledge that their guy was to the Laneites' guy as is the sun to a farthing candle.

Hubert approached William.

"She's not come yet," he said. "I said she was pulling our legs."

"It's not seven yet," said William.

Hubert looked curiously at the shrouded form of the Outlaws' guy.

"You'll take the cover off when she comes, I suppose?"

"Yes."

"And if she doesn't come, you'll take it off before you light your bonfire?"

"Yes."

The church clock struck seven:

"Come on," said William. "She said come and meet her down the road at seven."

"All right," said Hubert. "You go on, an' we'll come in a minute."

The Outlaws climbed the stile and set off down the road.

"We'll get it all right," said Ginger. "Theirs is the rottenest guy you ever saw. The sacking came off for a minute while they were putting it up, an' I saw it. It's *rotten*."

"There she is!"

"There's two of them," said Douglas.

"*Gosh!*" breathed William, stopping still in sudden dismay.

For down the dark lane were coming the little girl and a taller, larger figure, wheeling a hand-cart. As they drew nearer the terrible suspicion became a certainty. The taller, larger figure was that of the Outlaws' foe, Major Blake.

"Here they are, Daddy," called the little girl in a clear, confident voice. "I told them to come and meet us at seven."

The Major gave his late foes a somewhat sheepish smile of greeting.

"This young lady's insisted on my coming along to the ceremony," he said. "There's to be a bonfire and fireworks and prize-giving and midnight feast, I'm told. This"—he pointed to the hand-cart he was wheeling— "this is the midnight feast. She wouldn't let me have it sent on or bring it in the car in a civilised fashion!"

There was a strange new docility about the Major. From a roaring lion he had become the meekest of lambs. It was clear even to the Outlaws that he was his daughter's most humble and adoring slave.

"Of *course* Daddy had to come," she explained, slipping her arm affectionately through his. "It wouldn't be any fun at all without Daddy."

The Outlaws gasped at this amazing statement. The most amazing part of it was, of course, that it was made in good faith. Quite obviously the little girl honestly believed that it wouldn't be any fun at all without Daddy. The transformed Major smiled down at her fondly, then turned his sheepish grin once more upon the Outlaws.

"Look alive, young men," he said. "Here, you, carry the basket. And give a hand with the cart. Why should I be expected to do all the work?"

They walked along the lane towards the field, the Outlaws carrying the baskets and pushing the hand-cart. The little girl held a large square parcel under her arm that, she informed them, was the camera. She chattered eagerly as they went along, explaining to the Outlaws that she had been staying with an aunt till Daddy had got settled at the Hall, but now she had come to live with him, and that she loved the Hall and the village and the Outlaws and everything else in it.

The Outlaws listened absently and with growing feelings of consternation. The thought of the masterpiece of guydom on which they had spent such

time and labour filled them now, not with pride, but with
horror and dismay. They tried to imagine the face of the
little girl when her eyes fell upon the caricature of her
beloved Daddy, and even William's knees felt rather
unsteady at the thought. Moreover, there was Daddy
himself to be reckoned with. He would almost certainly
change from lamb to lion at the sight, and he still carried
the redoubtable stick.

Immediately the situation dawned on them the
Outlaws had given up all hope of the prize, but that was
the least of their fears. The anger of the guyed one, the
contempt of the guyed one's daughter, would be even
harder to bear than the loss of the prize. And it was too
late to remedy matters. They could do nothing but
stagger along under their burdens, steeling themselves
to their fate. They had reached the stile that led to the
field. The Hubert Laneites had not yet appeared.

"Well, we can't take this barrow over there," said the
Major. "I'll wheel it round to the gate, shall I?"

William agreed dejectedly and piloted the little girl
over the stile, followed by a disconsolate trail of
Outlaws.

The two covered guys still stood on the two piles.
Hubert Lane came forward to greet them, wearing a
fatuous smirk.

"Sorry we weren't in time to meet you," he said.
"We're all ready. Are you, William?"

William nodded morosely.

The little girl at once instituted herself master of the
ceremonies.

"Now take the coverings off your guys. Then when
I've seen them both, start the bonfires and fireworks.
You take yours off first, William."

William was conscious of a distinctly qualmy feeling in
the pit of his stomach as he stepped forward very slowly

and reluctantly. Very slowly and reluctantly he drew the sacking cover from the guy on the top of his bonfire. Then he stood gazing at it, open mouthed with amazement. It was not his guy at all. It was a paltry affair consisting of a halfpenny mask and an old coat. And at once he realised what had happened. Hubert, determined to win the prize at all costs, had secretly uncovered the Outlaws' guy while they had gone to meet the little girl, and, recognising its superiority, had put it on his own pile and substituted his own guy in its place. William walked back to the little girl, a curious smile on his face. The little girl examined it critically, her head on one side.

"Y-yes," she said, "it's *quite* good. I've seen lots of better guys, but it isn't bad. Now, Hubert, take the cover off yours."

Hubert advanced to his pile and removed the cover, then turned to the little girl with a triumphant grin. The little girl gazed at the guy. Then the smile dropped from her face, and horror and fury dawned upon it.

"You *hateful* boy!" she cried. "It's a horrible guy. I won't give you the prize whatever your old fireworks are like, and I won't have you or any of your hateful gang to my feast. So there!"

The bewildered Hubert stared at her, open mouthed.

"B-b-b-but——" he began.

The little girl interrupted him, stamping her foot angrily.

"How *dare* you make fun of my Daddy!" she said.

The truth dawned slowly upon Hubert.

"I didn't do it," he said eagerly. "It's not my guy." He pointed to William. "It's his."

"Don't tell such wicked stories," flamed the little girl. "Of *course* it's your guy. It's there on the top of your bonfire, and you took the cover off it when I told you to

"YOU *HATEFUL* BOY!" CRIED THE LITTLE GIRL. "HOW *DARE* YOU MAKE FUN OF MY DADDY?"

take the cover off your guy. Of course it's your guy. Don't take any notice of him, William. Don't even answer him."

William obeyed, preserving a masterly silence.

"I DIDN'T DO IT," SAID HUBERT, POINTING TO WILLIAM. "IT'S
NOT MY GUY. IT'S HIS."

"L-l-look here——" began Hubert in explanation,
but that was as far as he got, for at that moment the
Major, having wheeled his hand-cart of food into the old
barn, appeared upon the scene. He gazed at the red-

nosed, monocled, heavily moustached figure in the familiar brown suit, and his face grew purple with fury. The lamb had departed, leaving the lion once more in full possession.

"*They* did it, Daddy," said the little girl, pointing an accusing finger at Hubert and his gang.

With a bellow of anger the Major sprang at them. They fled in wild confusion, the vanguard receiving the full impact of the famous stick.

His punitive expedition accomplished, the Major returned to his daughter, a lamb once more.

"I'm so glad you've sent those horrible boys away," she said. "Here's the camera, William. Yours is heaps the best show. Now let's light your bonfire and then we'll go and have the feast. And if those horrible boys come back, Daddy will run after them with his stick again. . . . Now, light your bonfire, William."

With an expression of guileless innocence William stepped forward to light his bonfire. . . .

# Chapter 10

# William's Christmas Eve

William wandered slowly down the road. It was Christmas Eve, but the rush of preparation for Christmas was over. The presents he had prepared for his relations were safely wrapped up and put away in readiness for tomorrow. He had secretly discovered, examined and approved the presents that his relations had bought for him. There was nothing to do but to enjoy the afternoon, and he had arranged to do this by joining the Outlaws at a game of Red Indians in the woods.

He walked along whistling and swinging a stick he had taken from the hedgerows. But he was not thinking about the Outlaws or the game of Red Indians. He was thinking of Diana, the little girl who had recently arrived to live at the Hall with her father, Major Blake. She had shown distinct signs of favour to William, and the thought of her was beginning to come between him and his normal pursuits. As he walked along now, he was imagining that he met her at the bend of the road, that she stopped and talked to him, that she asked him to tea. . . .

He turned the bend of the road—and ran into her so violently that he almost knocked her down. She was not alone, however. She was with the tall, elderly, aristocratic-looking aunt who had arrived yesterday to spend Christmas at the Hall.

William apologised profusely. Diana smiled at him

sweetly. The aunt looked down her aristocratic nose.

"This is William," said Diana.

"How do you do?" said the aunt, holding out an aristocratic hand.

"Very well, thank you," said William, placing his grimy hand within it.

The aunt took out a handkerchief and carefully wiped a smear of mud from her grey kid gloves.

They passed on. Diana darted back.

"William," she whispered, "come round to the Hall's quick as you can. I'll be in the shrubbery. I want you to do something for me."

William's heart expanded in a warm glow of knight-errantry. At last his dreams were coming true. She wanted him to do something for her. . . .

He imagined himself killing dragons for her, fighting a thousand robbers single-handed, putting to flight hordes of savage beasts. He was in the act of slaying an imaginary dragon in the middle of the road when the other Outlaws came upon him. Somewhat sheepishly he abandoned his pugnacious attitude and picked up the stick with which he had just lunged at the invisible beast.

"What are you doing?" inquired Ginger.

"Jus' walkin' along," replied William coldly.

"Well, come on an' play Red Indians."

"I can't," said William. "I'm afraid I'm busy this afternoon."

"But you said you were coming."

"Well, I've changed my mind," said William. "I'm busy."

"Where are you going?"

"Never mind," said William. "I'm busy."

He walked on. Sadly they watched him turn into the field path that led to the Hall shrubbery.

"Red Indians is no fun without him," said Henry.

"It's that girl," said Ginger, shaking his head gloomily. "It's that girl."

They walked slowly on towards the woods. William, too, walked on a little more soberly. The meeting with the Outlaws had brought this soaring imagination back to earth. He realised that Diana could not possibly want him to kill a dragon or fight robbers and wild beasts. He realised this with regret, for he had always felt that he would distinguish himself in such contests.

"OH, *THERE* YOU ARE WILLIAM. I'M SO GLAD."

He reached the shrubbery and waited there patiently, concealed in the bushes. After some time Diana returned from her walk with her aunt and joined him.

"Oh, *there* you are, William! I'm so glad. I *knew* you'd come."

The note of admiration in her voice was gratifying.

"'*Course* I'd come," he said, swaggering as well as he could, considering that he was closely hemmed in by laurel bushes on all sides. "What d'you want me to do? I bet there's no one in the world I can't fight."

"Oh, I don't want you to fight anyone, William," she said.

His face fell. Even though it couldn't be dragons or wild beasts, he'd rather hoped it might be Hubert Lane or Bertie Franks or one of their gang.

"What d'you want me to do, then?" he said.

She drew nearer and sank her voice to a confidential whisper.

"Listen," she said. "It's Aunt Alex's Christmas present to me. It's a doll. I found it in one of her drawers, tied up in a parcel with 'To my dear little niece', written on it. And I *hate* dolls. I wanted a train."

William looked at her, bewildered. "Yes, but what can I do?" he said.

"I want you to steal it," said Diana. "Then she'll find it gone to-morrow, and it'll be too late to buy anything else, so she'll have to give me money, and I'll buy the train myself."

He gaped at her.

"But——" he began.

She interrupted him.

"I can't steal it. She'd be sure to see me coming out of her room with it. Or somebody would. Besides, I don't like telling really big stories, and it would be a really big story to say I didn't know anything about it if I'd done it

myself, and it would only be a little story to say I didn't
know anything about it if you'd done it."

William considered this point of view. There was
certainly something to be said for it. Still—he looked up
without enthusiasm at the enormous fortress-like house
into which he was expected to make a felonious
entrance—he'd far rather have fought someone. . . .

"Tell you what," he suggested at last. "You go up an'
get it and throw it out of the window to me, an' I'll take it
away."

Diana shook her head.

"No," she said slowly, "I don't want to do anything
myself. You see, I want to pretend to myself that I don't
know anything about it, and of course I can't do that if
I've thrown it out of the window to you."

"No, I suppose you can't," said William, once more
turning his eye upon the stately mansion and wishing it
had been a dragon. "Well, how can I get it?"

"It's quite easy," said Diana. "You can go up that
fire-escape staircase to the room at the corner there—
the one with the green curtains. That's her sitting-room,
and the bedroom's next door to it. The present's in the
drawer in the wardrobe. It's a square parcel with 'To my
dear little niece' written on it. You must get it and go
back to the sitting-room and come down the fire-escape
again. It's quite easy."

"Y-yes," agreed William doubtfully. "Er—s'pose
she's in her sitting-room."

"She won't be," said Diana. "And if she is you can
hide behind the curtains. They're long curtains that
come right down to the ground."

"Y-yes," said William again, still more doubtfully.
"Y-yes. An' suppose she comes into the bedroom while
I'm getting it."

"You must just make a dash for it," said Diana. "It's

quite easy. Of course"—her manner become rather chilly—"if you're *afraid* . . . "

"I'm not afraid," said William indignantly. "At least," as the memory of the tall, elderly, aristocratic-looking aunt returned to him, "I'm not afraid of robbers or wild beasts or that sort of thing. I say," he continued, after a thoughtful pause, "what's your aunt like when she's angry?"

"She's awful," said Diana darkly. "*Awful*. But don't worry. She won't catch you if you're quick."

"No, of course not," said William, and repeated, as if to reassure himself: "Of course not." After another thoughtful pause he continued: "P'raps I'd better not do it. For your sake, I mean," he added hastily. "I mean, if she catches me you'll get into a row for setting me on to it."

Diana looked at him with large surprised eyes.

"Oh, no, I won't," she assured him. "I shall say that I'd no idea that you were going to do it, and even if you say I told you to do it I shall say I didn't. Because, you see, I'm pretending to myself that I don't know anything about it. So you needn't be afraid of me getting into a row."

"N-no," said William, and, in spite of the removal of this anxiety, he looked strangely despondent. "N-no. I'm jolly glad about that, of course." Again he considered deeply and finally remarked: "You know, it might be an awfully nice doll."

"I hate dolls."

"Yes, but I mean, if you tried playing with this one you might like it. Lots of girls do like dolls, you know."

Again she looked at him coldly.

"If you don't want to do a little thing like this for me . . . " she said, and added reproachfully: "I thought you liked me."

"I do," said William earnestly. "Honest, I do." The coldness and reproach of the little girl's glance spurred him on to superhuman daring. "I'll go'n' get it now. Just watch me. I'll be down with it in two shakes."

Without waiting to consider, he hurried through the shrubbery, up the fire-escape, and in at the open window where the green curtains swayed in the breeze. Then he drew a deep breath and looked about him. It was a pleasant, fair-sized sitting-room, fortunately empty. From it a door led into the next room, which was presumably the bedroom. William, still upheld by his impulse of daring, was just making his way across the room to this door when he heard the sound of voices approaching and the handle of the door was turned. Swift as lightning he returned to the shelter of the curtains and stood concealed behind them. The aunt entered, accompanied by her Pekinese and a visitor.

"Yes," said the aunt, "it's a nice little room. A nice view, too."

They came over to the window and stood so close to William that he thought they must hear his heart beating.

Then they went to sit by the fire, leaving William in peace. But the peace was short-lived, for almost immediately the Pekinese discovered William's feet, which protruded from the bottom of the curtain. He fell upon them with a ferocious growl and began to worry them. William managed with difficulty to strangle the "Ow!" that was his natural reaction to this proceeding. The growls grew louder.

"What's the matter with Peky?" said the visitor.

The aunt threw a careless glance over her shoulder.

"Oh, he must have found his indiarubber bone. He'll worry it like that by the hour, the darling!"

They returned to their conversation, and the Pekinese

to his self-imposed task of tearing the socks from William's skin, and the skin from his ankles. William had reached the point at which discovery was preferable to further torture, when the aunt and the visitor rose and went out, the aunt calling "Peky!" over her shoulder.

William had the satisfaction of getting in a fairly good kick at his tormentor as it departed reluctantly, still snarling defiance at the two strange intruders who had appeared so unexpectedly beneath the curtain.

William heaved a sigh of relief as the door closed on them. The coast was clear at last. But the episode had shaken his nerve and destroyed the first fine careless rapture of bravado in which he had undertaken the adventure. He stayed for some minutes in the window embrasure, trying once more to screw up his courage to make the dash for the bedroom. He had just managed to screw it up—partially, at any rate—when he heard the sounds of the aunt and visitor returning, accompanied by the Pekinese. The aunt and the visitor he might have endured, but the thought of the Pekinese, who would, of course, immediately seek out again his late victims, completed the breaking of his nerve, and he climbed lightly out of the window, and proceeded farther up the fire-escape. It led to an open window which he regarded hopefully till he caught a glimpse of a maid arranging her cap before a mirror. He hurried on and found himself upon the roof.

It was a much-gabled roof, and he decided to explore it while he had the opportunity. He had reached the summit of the first gable when he was startled by the sound of voices and realised that the aunt and visitor had come out on to the balcony. He froze rigid on his gable.

"Yes, I really ought to have shown you the view from here," the aunt was saying. "It's a wonderful view."

"Wonderful," agreed the visitor vaguely. She gazed

round till her eyes finally rested upon William. "What a quaint old gargoyle up there on the roof!" she commented. "I'm short-sighted, of course, but to me from here it looks a delightfully quaint piece of work."

William hastily slid down from his gable-point to a hollow of the roof. The aunt found her *lorgnettes* and slowly turned them on to the gable.

"No, dear," she said at last, "it's just a tree-top that you see."

"I suppose so," said the friend in rather a perplexed fashion. "Of course I *am* very short-sighted. . . . It certainly seems to have gone from where it was."

"It's a tree-top moving in the wind," explained the aunt.

They disappeared into the house. So shattered was William's nerve by this time that, though he had by no means abandoned the enterprise, he decided not to return to the fire-escape, but to try to make a less obtrusive entrance from the roof. After clambering about for some time he discovered a chimney that seemed to be large and smokeless and accommodating. He was just peering into it hopefully when a gust of sooty smoke caught him in the face. He withdrew, choking. Someone had evidently just lit the fire. He continued his exploration till he came to a skylight. He opened it and began to let himself down gently into the room below, receiving somewhat of a shock as he felt his legs dangling into a tank of ice-cold water. He wriggled away from it and at last dropped on to the ground clear of it, bruising himself considerably in the process. Limping slightly from the combined effect of the Pekinese and the fall, he went along a passage and down a staircase. Fortune seemed suddenly to favour him, for the staircase led to the landing just outside the sitting-room with the green curtains.

He darted into it and through the door into the bedroom. He opened the drawer, found the parcel, and dashed back into the sitting-room. Unfortunately a maid had just come in to put coals on the fire. She gazed at the limping, black-faced, dripping apparition, then gave a

**THE MAID GAVE A YELL AND FLED.**

yell and fled. William slipped down the fire-escape, still clutching his parcel, and joined the little girl in the shrubbery.

"Oh, William, how *dreadful* you look!" she greeted him with distaste.

"Can't help it," panted William. "It was a chimney

and a water-tank. . . . Here's the parcel."

She took it, and a smile of triumph dawned slowly on her face.

"Oh, William, *thank* you," she said. "I *knew* you'd get it . . . and I've got a reward for you. I've asked aunt if you may come to tea, and she says you may. But you look *awful*, William. You'll have to get tidy, or I know she won't let you stay to tea. And the parcel . . . . she mustn't find that. What'll we do with it?"

"*I* know," said William. "Our gardener's got a fire. I'll go home an' burn it an' get tidy for comin' to tea with you."

"Oh, *yes,* William," said the little girl eagerly. "Oh, William, you are *clever*. And you are brave, too. I shall never forget how you went straight up the fire-escape to get that parcel."

"Oh, that's nothin'," murmured William complacently. "Nothin' at all."

"Well, you'd better be quick, William," urged Diana. "It would be *awful* if aunt caught you all black and wet like that, and with the parcel."

Realising this, William set off homeward as quickly as possible.

In about half an hour he returned, still limping, but spick and span and without the parcel.

"I've burnt it," he said. "I've burnt it till there wasn't anything at all of it left. An' I've made myself jolly tidy, haven't I?"

"Yes, you *have*," said the little girl admiringly. "William, I think you're *wonderful*!"

At this moment the aunt issued from the front door and came across the lawn to them. She was carrying a large parcel under her arm.

"Is this the little friend you're having to tea?" she asked.

"Yes," said Diana.

The aunt looked at William rather coldly.

"Well, don't get rough," she said. "I'll be back by tea-time, but I just have to go to the post office." She turned to Diana. "I hope you don't mind, dear. I'm afraid I shall have to send the train I'd got for you to your little cousin Dorita. I'd got a doll for her, but when I went to look for it just now it wasn't there. I suppose I must have forgotten to bring it. So I'm sending her your train. I'm sure you won't mind, dear, will you? I've got a nice book that I know you'd like instead. Stories from English History. I can't send that to Dorita because I sent it to her last year. But I'm certain you'll like it, and won't grudge her your train. And you'll play quietly till I come back, won't you?"

She swept on down the drive. There was a tense silence.

Then the little girl turned on William, her small face pink with anger.

"It's all your fault, you hateful boy! You took it and burnt it, and now I've got to have a rotten old history book instead of my train. . . . I *hate* you."

William blinked at her in amazement.

"B-b-but you told me to," he stammered.

The little girl stamped her foot.

"Don't keep *arguing* about it," she stormed. "It's *all* your fault. You burnt the doll, and so I've got to have a rotten old history book instead of my train. I hope someone burns up all your presents like you've burnt up mine. And go away. I don't want you. I don't ever want to see you again as long as I live. . . . "

\*      \*      \*

The Outlaws, engaged in a not very successful game of Red Indians—for no game seemed really successful

"IT'S ALL YOUR FAULT," DIANA STORMED. "I DON'T EVER
WANT TO SEE YOU AGAIN AS LONG AS I LIVE."

when William was not there—were surprised and
secretly relieved to see William coming through the
wood to join them. He still limped slightly and looked
tidier than usual, though already a good deal of the

spick-and-spanness achieved for his visit to the little girl had fallen from him.

"Hello," said Ginger. "Have you hurt your foot?"

"No," said William. "I'm pretending to be a lame Red Indian that was nearly killed by a bear."

"Thought you weren't coming," said Douglas.

William assumed an expression of rather cold surprise.

"Not coming?" he said. "Why shouldn't I be coming?"

"I thought you were going to that girl."

"What girl?" countered William.

"Diana Blake," said Ginger.

William appeared to search deeply in his memory.

"Oh, *that* girl," he said, as if a faint memory had emerged from the far distant past. "*That* girl. Good gracious, no! I've finished with her for ever. I've finished with all girls for ever. . . . Come on. Let's start playing Red Indians."

# Chapter 11

# A Night of Mysteries

Robert opened the envelope, took out the printed card and studied it with obviously rising excitement.

"What is it, dear?" said his mother.

"An invitation," replied Robert excitedly. "An invitation to a fancy dress dance on New Year's Eve at Hadley Grange. I say, isn't that jolly?"

"Yes," said Mrs. Brown. "But what a pity Ethel's away for it!"

"Um, I shall have to go alone." Then he studied the card more carefully and his excitement waned. "Good Lord!" he groaned; "William's invited!"

"How nice for him," commented Mrs. Brown placidly.

"For him—yes," said Robert with a bitter laugh.

"And for you, too," said his mother with still unruffled placidity. "You'll have someone to go with."

Robert was silent for a few moments, considering his mode of attack. Then he said:

"Yes, of course I'd like him to go with, but honestly, Mother, I don't think you ought to let him go. I mean, a fancy dress dance is no place for a kid."

"But why, dear?" said Mrs. Brown. "He's been invited, and he's got a very nice Red Indian costume. Why shouldn't he go?"

"Because he'll jolly well mess everything up," said Robert, abandoning finesse. "It's no use asking me why he'll mess everything up because I don't know. I never do know. I only know that he always does."

"Nonsense, dear," said Mrs. Brown. "He sometimes makes mistakes, of course, but he always means well. Oh, here he is."

William entered the room and, being told of the invitation, proceeded to display much virtuous indignation at Robert's attitude.

"Me?" he said. "I've never messed anything up. Ever. I don't know what he's talking about."

Reminded of various occasions when his well-meant interference had further complicated situations that were complicated enough to begin with, William took refuge in an attitude of dignified reproach.

"You jus' don't want me to have any pleasure at all, that's what it is," he said. "You jus' want me to go on havin' a hard time all my life with no pleasure at all."

"A hard time!" jeered Robert, but Mrs. Brown hastily interposed.

"Now that's enough, children. Of course, William must go to the fancy dress dance as he's been invited, and I'm sure he'll be nice company for you, Robert."

Robert gave a sardonic and provocative snort, but William, having gained his point, ignored it.

"What shall I go as?" he asked his mother.

"Why not a Red Indian?" she suggested. "You've got such a nice Red Indian costume."

"That ole thing!" said William scornfully.

"*Most* suitable," commented Robert as if to himself.

"I'd rather be a Red Indian than you any day," said William, stung by the dispassionate irony of Robert's tone.

"Yes, dear," put in Mrs. Brown, vaguely conciliatory, "Red Indians are very nice, and Robert's very nice. Each in their own way, of course. We could get

"YOU JUS' DON'T WANT ME TO HAVE ANY PLEASURE AT ALL.
THAT'S WHAT IT IS," SAID WILLIAM.

more feathers for your head-dress, you know, William,
and it would quite smarten up the costume."

William, who in reality had a secret affection for his
old Red Indian suit, was content with this, and haunted
the farm-yards of the neighbourhood for several days,
picking up feathers, and even forcibly depriving several
indignant hens of the chief ornaments of their tails. He

then turned his attention to Robert's costume. Robert, he discovered, had decided to go to the dance as a pierrot. William, considering that this showed an unworthy lack of enterprise, suggested various alternatives, such as gorilla, bloodhound, lion-tamer, or chimney-sweep, and expended all his powers of persuasion on the subject, but Robert remained unmoved by his eloquence, and Mrs. Brown, with the help of a paper pattern, evolved an elaborate affair of wide frills and enormous black velvet buttons that Robert secretly considered extremely becoming.

They were to go to Hadley in the two-seater that had once been the pride and joy of Robert's heart, but was now in reality more of an anxiety than a pride or joy. Though, thanks to Robert's ceaseless care, its outside still gleamed and shone with polished metal and constantly renewed green and yellow paint of a somewhat bilious shade, its inside had developed an unreliability that was apt to display itself at the most inopportune moments. Robert had, in fact, almost made up his mind not to risk its breaking down on the way to the fancy dress dance, but to order a taxi instead, when William happened to remark:

"Well, anyway, I hope we aren't going in Robert's ole car."

"Why not?" asked Robert with icy dignity.

"Well, you know what it is," said William succinctly.

"And what is it?" demanded Robert with a still more icy dignity.

"Well, it broke down three times last week, didn't it?" asked William in a tone of sweet reasonableness.

"It didn't break down once," said Robert with the cold fury that any disparagement of his car always roused in him. "I stopped it once or twice in order to make minor adjustments, that's all. Of course we're going to the fancy dress dance in it. It's far more reliable than a taxi."

So the two of them set off in Robert's car, Robert wearing his be-frilled pierrot costume, William his Red Indian suit.

William preserved a masterly silence when the car came slowly and jerkily to a stop on a lonely stretch of road. Robert started it again. It leaped forward jerkily, wheezed, then stopped again. Once more Robert started it. Once more it rocked and wheezed and jerked, but this time did not start. Robert got out of it, his face set and desperate, remarking casually:

"It just wants a minor adjustment, I expect."

He disappeared into the engine for a few minutes, then returned to his seat and pressed the starting-button. A loud grating sound followed, the car leapt forward, then came once more to a sudden stop. Robert got out of it again.

"Are you going to do another minor adjustment?" asked William. Without replying Robert dived beneath the car and there followed various tremors and rattles and bangs, punctuated by gasps from the desperate Robert.

After a few minutes he returned to his seat, outwardly calm.

"I think it will be all right now," he said casually.

He pressed the starting-button, and once more the car bucked wildly as if determined to unseat its two occupants, but made no further progress along the road. Yet again Robert got out and dived beneath it. Again William listened to the rattle and jerks of machinery, punctuated by Robert's resolute and stertorous breathing. At last, with a set, stern face whose impressiveness was somewhat marred by a long streak of black oil, he resumed his seat.

"Now I think I've settled it all right," he remarked, as he pressed the starting-button.

He had certainly settled it in that he had cowed it into utter subjection. Its power of resistance was completely gone. It moaned feebly when the starting-button was pressed, but no longer struggled, or even, beyond a slight quiver, stirred.

Again Robert leapt out and turned the starting-handle. Like the rest of the car it was cowed into subjection. It swung round and round as easily and ineffectively as the handle of a defunct barrel-organ. Robert stood and glared desperately down at the green and yellow midget.

His once white pierrot suit was crumpled, mud-stained and streaked heavily with black oil, but of this he was for the moment mercifully unaware.

"It's probably something quite simple," he remarked with an unconvincing attempt at nonchalance, "if only one knew what it was. Quite a minor adjustment. I mean, it's a very good little car."

William again broke his masterly silence.

"It's not really very far to walk from here," he said.

A few moments ago Robert would have treated the suggestion as a deliberate and unpardonable insult, but by this time his spirit as well as the car's was broken, and his oil-streaked face lit up at the idea.

"Why, of course it isn't," he said, then his eyes fell upon his costume, and his face froze into a mask of horror. "But I can't possibly go like this. I can't *possibly*."

"There's a stream jus' by the roadside," suggested William. "Couldn't you clean up a bit there?"

"Don't be ridiculous," said Robert, feeling a certain relief in venting his anger upon someone. "Don't be so utterly ridiculous. No," he went on tragically, "I can't go, that's all there is to it. I just can't go. You'd better go on alone."

William's face grew as purposeful as Robert's was tragic. William was determined to go to the fancy dress dance, and he was determined that Robert should go too. The catastrophe that had made Robert abandon hope had roused all William's fighting spirit. He knit his freckled brows fiercely. There must be a way if only one could think of it. Even William, on serious reflection, realised that the pierrot costume was past hope. There was hardly a square inch of it left in its pristine state of purity. It was crumpled beyond recognition and literally covered by oil and mud. Still—William wrinkled his freckled brows again—there *must* be a way. Though there were few houses near, one of them might contain an occupant who combined an exhaustive knowledge of the mechanism of small cars coupled with a kind heart.

"Shall I just go and see if anyone in those houses can do anything?" he suggested.

Robert, who had a strong sense of personal dignity, was horrified by the suggestion.

"Of course not," he said indignantly. "I should never be able to look anyone in the face again for the rest of my life if you did a thing like that."

"Why not?" asked William simply. "I mean, why wouldn't you be able to look anyone in the face again for the rest of your life if I did that?"

Robert, who knew that it was useless to expect an understanding of the finer shades of delicacy of feeling from William, merely shrugged his shoulders and said:

"Well, you'd better be getting on or you'll be late. Tell them I'm ill." He glared balefully at William. "Don't mention the car or I'll never speak to you again. Say I've got 'flu."

"'Flu's a bit ordinary," said William, giving his whole attention now to the subject of Robert's excuse. "S'pose I say you've got pneumonia or heart disease or something a bit more interesting."

"Do as you're told," snapped Robert angrily. "Say I've got 'flu."

It was evident that Robert was bitterly disappointed and humiliated by what had happened. And again William summoned up all his powers of determination and ingenuity. There *must* be a way. . . . He glanced around at the dark winter landscape. Lights shone through the trees here and there, showing a few scattered houses.

"Jus' wait a minute. I won't be long," he called, and set off suddenly at a run down the road.

"Hi!" called Robert. "Where are you going?"

There came no answer. Robert stood dejectedly for a few moments by his mutinous pet, then set to work in a frenzy of despair, flooding the carburettor, winding the starting-handle, pressing the starting-button, taking out the plugs, putting them back, taking them out again, putting them back. . . . Beyond an occasional moan his victim gave no sign of life.

William ran on down the dark road. There was no definite plan in his mind, but he trusted to Fate to find some way for him. After all, anything was possible. He might meet a man with a car and a fancy dress who would stop him and ask him if he knew anyone who would like to borrow them for the evening as he suddenly remembered another engagement. It was soon obvious, however, that this was not going to happen. The road was completely deserted except for himself. He glanced at the lights of the houses that could be seen through the trees and played for a few moments with the idea of going up to one of the front doors and asking if the master of the house would be so kind as to lend him a motor-car and a fancy dress costume—or at any rate a fancy dress costume. But even William's courage failed at the thought of actually doing this.

He had now reached the end of the road. There was a small pub there, and outside the pub was a motor-cycle whose occupant was evidently inside the pub having a drink. William gazed at the motor-cycle longingly. He would have liked to "borrow" it for Robert's use, but Robert, he knew, would refuse indignantly to accept such a "loan". And even if he did it would not solve the problem of the fancy dress. . . . A brown-paper parcel was tied on to the back of the motor-cycle. William examined it. Through a small tear in the brown paper a piece of gaily-striped material could be seen. William's interest grew. Surely some sort of fancy dress costume could be evolved for Robert from a piece of gaily-striped material. He must at any rate satisfy his curiosity. Probably the owner of the cycle would be staying in the pub for some time. There wouldn't be any harm in his taking off the parcel and going to the nearest street lamp just to see what it was. He'd have put it back again on the motor-cycle before the owner came out. He glanced up and down the road. No one was in sight. Swiftly he untied the parcel from the carrier and hurried down the road with it to the street lamp. Very cautiously he opened the brown paper and inspected the contents. Then he drew in his breath sharply. It was almost incredible, but there it was before his very eyes. The parcel contained a complete harlequin's costume with a short cloak to match. It was a gift from Fate. There were no other ways of looking at it—for William, at any rate. He bundled it up under his arm and ran down to Robert, who arose, blacker than ever, from beneath the car to greet him.

"Where on *earth* have you been?" he demanded testily.

Panting, William held out the costume.

"Look," he said simply. "I've got you this."

Robert gazed at it, open mouthed with amazement.

"But w-where have you got it from?" he stammered.

William's mind worked quickly. Robert had a hopelessly conventional outlook upon life. If he told Robert where he had got it from, Robert would insist on his taking it back at once. No, Robert must be deceived for his own good.

"Well," he said slowly, "jus' as I was goin' up the road, I saw a man at a gate an' he sort of spoke to me. I mean, he asked me what I was doin' an' that sort of thing an' I told him we were goin' to a fancy dress dance but you'd got your pierrot costume all dirty mending the car on the road"—mending, thought William complacently, was a tactful touch—"an' that you were afraid you'd have to go home instead, an' he said he'd got this ole costume upstairs that he never used an' he said he'd lend it us with pleasure, an' so he fetched it down and gave it me."

Robert gazed at the costume in an amazement that changed gradually to an ecstasy of joy and relief.

"I say, did he *really*?"

"Yes," said William, who as usual had by now begun to believe his own story and, indeed, had a vivid memory of a small, kindly, white-haired man standing at the gate of a house and offering Robert a fancy dress costume.

"But I *say*!" gasped the credulous Robert. "How *kind* of him!"

"Yes, wasn't it?" agreed William.

"Which house was it?"

"Er—the one at the corner," said William.

"I know. It's called The Elms, isn't it?"

"I *think* it is," said William guardedly, "but I'm not quite sure."

"Yes, it is. I know it is," said Robert eagerly. "I say, it *is* decent of him. I'll just run and thank him before I put it on."

"No, you mustn't," said William urgently. "Honest, you mustn't."

"Why not?"

"I can't explain," said William. "I mean—well, you mustn't. He said most particular you mustn't."

"But why not?" demanded Robert.

"Well——" William's face looked set and tense as he searched for a convincing reason why Robert should not return and thank the occupant of The Elms for lending him a fancy dress costume. "Well, for one reason he hates being thanked. He said most particular that he hated being thanked."

"Yes, but in a case like *this* . . . " persisted Robert.

A seraphic smile lit up William's face as a flash of inspiration came to him.

"Well, you see, he said he was an author an' he was very busy trying to get to the end of a chapter in his book—the one where they catch the villain, you know—and he's alone in the house, an' has to answer the door himself an' he said most particular that he mustn't be disturbed jus' 'cause of that."

"Oh, yes," said Robert reverently (Robert had a deep respect for authors). "Yes, of course I quite understand. I certainly won't go round there now if that's the case. But I'll go round first thing to-morrow to thank him."

"Oh, yes, that'll be all right," said William, who always believed in letting to-morrow take care of itself. Sufficient, and more than sufficient generally, in William's opinion, to the day was the evil thereof.

"Well, I'd better change quickly," said Robert, whose depression and irritability had now given place to excitement, "or we shall be late."

William subjected him to a dispassionate scrutiny.

"You'd better clean up your face a bit, hadn't you?" he suggested.

"Yes, of course," said Robert, his depression returning, "but how on earth am I going to do it?"

William remembered a small tube of grease solvent that had been sent with the car and that still reposed at the bottom of the tool-box. He took it out, led Robert to the stream, and, using the clean handkerchief that Mrs. Brown had carefully put into the pocket of his Red Indian suit, made a fairly satisfactory job of Robert's face. Then Robert withdrew into the recesses of the car to change from the pierrot suit that now closely resembled a pair of garage overalls to the harlequin costume. He conversed animatedly with William as he did so.

"I say, you know, it *was* decent of him."

"Yes, wasn't it?" agreed William.

"Was he an old man?"

"Sort of old in a way," said William.

"If this was his he must have been quite thin. It only just goes on me."

"Oh, yes," agreed William, "he was thin all right."

"What luck that you just met him at the gate!"

"Yes, wasn't it?"

"What was he doing there? Posting a letter?"

"Yes. He was sort of posting a letter."

"Well, I think it was *jolly* kind of him. Lending a fancy dress costume to someone you've never seen in your life before! I don't think many people would do that."

"No, I don't either."

"For all he knows, we'll never take it back."

"I'll take it back all right. You needn't worry about

taking it back. I'll see to that."

"Oh, I must take it back and thank him in person, of course," said Robert.

"He said he was going away very early to-morrow morning," said William with another burst of inspiration. "Somewhere a long way off. Jerusalem or somewhere like that. So it's no use you going. I'll just take it there and leave it with a note, shall I?"

Robert was now completely clothed as a harlequin. The stripes seemed to run in rather odd directions, but it was a well-made, well-fitting costume, with a cloak and a mask that hid all his features but his chin.

"It's *jolly* fine, isn't it?" he said in great delight. "It's really much better than the pierrot suit. It certainly was *jolly* decent of that man at The Elms."

"Come on," said William, who, now that Robert had actually put on the costume, was nervously scanning the landscape, fearful of the arrival of an indignant motor-cyclist demanding his fancy dress suit from a bewildered Robert. "Let's get off quickly or we'll be late."

"All right," said Robert. "I'll leave the car here. They can fetch it from the garage in the morning."

They set off, walking quickly through the darkness in the direction of Hadley, William still casting nervous glances around and deciding that flight was the only resource should the indignant motor-cyclist descend on them. No indignant motor-cyclist, however, descended, and they reached Hadley Grange in safety.

Robert at once sought out such local belles as he happened at the moment to admire, and William went off in search of his friends, with whom he made an early and prolonged visit to the refreshment buffet. The two did not meet again till some time later, when William happened to be passing through the hall, and Robert happened to be standing with a group round the fire.

William's attention was caught by the words "The Elms", and he froze suddenly into immobility.

"Yes," a thick-set, middle-aged man, dressed as a pirate, was saying, "I've simply given up trying to do anything with my garden. It's shut in by trees on all sides."

"The—The Elms, did you say?" stammered Robert eagerly.

The thick-set, middle-aged man, who had been addressing a group of his contemporaries, turned upon Robert with a scowl, as if resenting the intrusion of this unknown youth into the conversation.

"Yes, The Elms," he said shortly.

"The house at the corner of the common?" went on Robert.

"Yes," snapped the pirate.

"Oh, I say!" burbled Robert in an ecstasy of gratitude. "You see what I'm wearing, don't you? I'm so glad to have this opportunity of thanking you."

The pirate gazed at him blankly.

"Don't know what you're talking about," he snapped.

Robert remembered that William had said he didn't want to be thanked. A good many kind-hearted people were like that, of course.

He drew his harlequin's cape around him and glanced down at his gaily striped legs.

"It fits me quite well, doesn't it?" he said.

The pirate's scowl deepened to a glare.

"Does it?" he said. "I really haven't noticed."

Evidently he was sensitive about any reference to his generosity. Robert changed the subject.

"I hear you're making an early start for Jerusalem to-morrow morning," he said pleasantly.

The pirate flushed angrily.

"What on *earth* are you talking about?" he said.

He evidently didn't want people to know that he was going to Jerusalem, either, thought Robert. Still—he was burning to prove his gratitude by showing a friendly interest in his benefactor's concerns. .

"I hope you managed to catch the villain before you set off this evening?" he went on.

The pirate's face was suffused with an angry purple, but before he could speak one of Robert's belles appeared at the door of the dance-room, beckoning to him, and Robert leapt dutifully to obey the signal. The pirate gazed round the circle, his face still flushed with anger.

"Is that young man mad or merely impudent?" he said to the assembled circle.

But the assembled circle, though faintly amused and mystified, was not really interested in the subject. The music of the next dance was striking up, and the circle moved slowly towards the dance-room. Only the pirate was left. He stood for a few moments scowling ferociously in front of him, then he, too, started abruptly towards the dance-room, but with the mien of one about, not to dance, but to demand the explanation of an insult.

With the courage of despair William barred his way.

"'Scuse me," he said with a mixture of urgency and politeness, "but are you going to speak to that man in the striped dress?"

"Yes, I am," snarled the pirate. "I've never been made game of in public before, and I'm not going to start now. Who is he, anyway?"

"He's my brother," said William breathlessly, "an' I jus' wanted to explain about him. He didn't mean anything by those things he said to you."

"Didn't mean anything!" sputtered the pirate. "Talking about making an early start for Jerusalem!

"'SCUSE ME," SAID WILLIAM, "BUT ARE YOU GOING TO SPEAK
TO THAT MAN IN THE STRIPED DRESS?"

Asking me if I'd caught the villain! If he isn't mad he
wants horse-whipping for his impudence."

"He's not *exactly* mad," said William thoughtfully,
"but he's had brain-fever, an' it makes him say funny
things like that. But he doesn't mean anything. He
doesn't, honest."

The pirate looked taken aback.

"Surely he oughtn't to be going about among people
if that's the case."

"Oh, yes," said William, "the doctor says he can go about among people. He says it's good for him. But he says no one must get angry with him or ask him what he means by the things he says or else he might go mad quite sudden."

The pirate returned to the fire, still scowling moodily.

"I saw at once that it was either impudence or mental trouble," he said. "If it's mental trouble, I'm sorry for the boy, of course."

"Yes, it's mental trouble all right," said William. "I'm sorry for him, too."

"But I certainly think he ought to be kept quiet at home."

"Yes, so do I," agreed William. "I'll tell my mother you think so."

Meantime in an alcove of the dance-room the unconscious Robert was sitting out the dance with the belle of the moment.

"Isn't it *hot* in here!" said the belle.

"Yes . . . let's try and find a cooler place somewhere, shall we?" said Robert solicitously.

"Oh, no," said the belle. "I like watching them dance. Some of them simply can't dance for nuts, can they? Of course, I know I can't myself"—she paused for Robert to murmur the appropriate contradiction—"but—well, I'm better than one or two of them. *Isn't* it hot? I'd love an ice, wouldn't you?"

"I'll get you one," said Robert, springing to his feet.

To reach the buffet he had to cross the hall. The pirate still stood in front of the fire. Robert gave him a grateful, friendly, conspiratorial smile as he passed—the smile of the benefited to the benefactor who does not wish to have the benefit mentioned. The pirate shook his head sadly as Robert vanished from view.

The buffet was at the end of the passage. Robert

walked gaily towards it. Then—when he had almost reached it, a man stepped out of the shadow of a curtain and confronted him.

He was a large, burly man, dressed harmlessly enough as Henry the Eighth, but something about his face made Robert's blood suddenly run cold. It was a rough-hewn, savage, lowering sort of face. A mask hid the eyes, but the mouth was an aggressive, ferocious slit. He spoke in a voice that matched his face.

"How much longer did you want me to wait for you? I thought you were never coming. You're five minutes late. Do you know that?"

Robert gaped helplessly.

"B-but I say——" he began at last. Henry the Eighth interrupted him savagely.

"Well, come on now you're here and don't waste time jabbering. Follow me and don't make a noise or I'll wring your neck. I've got the goods, see?"

Looking down, Robert saw that the other man held a small pistol in one hand. The hair on Robert's head seemed to raise itself slowly and stand on end. Cold shivers crept up and down his spine.

"Come on," rasped the man and began to creep down a passage at right-angles to the one that led to the buffet. Hypnotised by horror, Robert followed. The man crept up a small winding back staircase. Still hypnotised by horror, Robert still followed. Once a stair creaked beneath him, and the man turned on him with a silent snarl that made Robert's teeth chatter audibly. Cautiously, noiselessly, the man opened the door of a bedroom and entered. Robert followed. Moving with almost incredible rapidity considering his bulk, the man went to a picture on the wall, did something to it with a small wire instrument, then swung it back, revealing a hidden safe. Then he turned suddenly on Robert, speaking in a low, threatening tone.

"Come on here, you darned lout! Why are you standing gaping? I've never known the chief send me such a fool before to help in a job. Where's your bag?"

"I—I—I——" stammered Robert wildly.

"Here!" said the man impatiently, snatching up an attaché-case that stood in a corner of the room. "Here, use this. The chief must be barmy, that's all I can say. Look sharp, now. Hold it open."

Robert obeyed, and the man emptied into it the gleaming contents of a jewel-case whose lock he had been picking with quick, deft movements as he spoke.

"That's all we want here. We'll take it down to the car, then you get off on your motor-bike back to the chief and report. Here, you carry it. You're a better runner than me if we're set on. Go on in front of me and remember I've got a gun if you try any funny tricks."

Trembling, Robert set off with the stolen jewels in front of the man. He could hear him breathing heavily just behind him. He could feel the pistol against the small of his back. The whole thing was like a nightmare. The pistol propelled him down the staircase, out at a small side door, and on through what was evidently a kitchen garden. Occasionally Robert tripped over bushes and plants in the darkness, and the man behind cursed him softly but eloquently. The perspiration was standing out on Robert's brow and trickling down his nose.

Suddenly an uproar arose in the distance, shouts were heard, and lights seen through the trees.

"Let's search the shrubbery," shouted a voice. "They may be there."

"They've probably got off."

"Have they taken much?"

"All Moyna's jewels. Her maid's just gone to the

ROBERT FOUND HIMSELF IN THE MIDDLE OF AN EXCITED
CROWD.

room and found the safe opened."

"It's your fault for being late, you darned fool,"
hissed the man. "Five minutes would have made all the
difference. Take the stuff down to the road through the
park—none of them are on the park side—and drive off
the car before the police get here. You're a better runner
than me and they're less likely to see you. Here, put this

"IT WAS SPLENDID OF YOU, ROBERT," SOMEBODY SAID.

on." He threw his dark cloak over Robert's gaily striped costume. "Drive straight to the chief. I'll follow. *Get* on, can't you?"

Another jab in the ribs with the pistol emphasised the order, and Robert set off, running through the darkness. He didn't know where the park was. He didn't know where the car was. He didn't know where anything was. He was running simply to get away from the man with the pistol. His cloak came off, his mask came off. Still he ran on.

Suddenly he found himself in the middle of a group of people. Excited voices arose on all sides.

"Why, it's Robert."

"It's Robert Brown."

"He's got the case."

"It's the jewels."

"Robert's got the *jewels*."

"Robert, how splendid of you! How *did* you manage it?"

"I say, Robert's caught the thief. He's got the jewels."

"Where's the thief, Robert?"

Panting, gasping, Robert pointed vaguely behind him.

"He's probably got off now," said someone, "and anyway now we've got the jewels back it doesn't matter so much."

"Is everything there that was taken, Moyna?"

"Yes, everything."

"I say, Robert, it was splendid of you to tackle him alone. Absolutely *splendid*. Where did you find him?"

"Poor boy, he can hardly speak. He must have had an awful fight. He'll tell us all about it later, won't you, Robert?"

Robert nodded.

"The poor boy's absolutely done in."

"Take him to have a drink. Then he can tell us all about it when he feels better."

Willing hands assisted Robert to the hall, installed him in an armchair by the fire, and supplied him with restoratives. He was beginning to feel slightly better.

"Take your time, old boy," said a reassuring voice. "You can tell us the whole story in a minute or two, but don't try to do it yet. . . . Here, fill up his glass again, somebody."

Somebody filled up his glass again. Yes, he was certainly feeling better. He'd certainly be ready to tell them the whole story in a minute or two. He'd never be able to make them understand it, though. He didn't understand it himself. Suddenly he dismissed it. It was absurd. It couldn't possibly have happened. No, the real facts must have been quite different.

"Well, you see," he began slowly, "I was just on my way to the buffet and just happened to step out on to the lawn for a breath of fresh air when I saw this chap skulking through the trees with the case, so without thinking at all I ran after him and set on him. I sort of knew he was a thief. There was a bit of a fight, of course," he concluded modestly, "but he soon ran off. . . . "

A babble of hero-worshipping voices arose from all sides of him. The man who had lent him the costume was shaking him warmly by the hand.

"I'm sorry I was a bit short with you earlier this evening," he said. "After you'd gone your brother told me about your illness."

"My illness?" gasped Robert, a helpless sense of bewilderment descending on him once more.

"Yes, whatever else it's affected, it certainly hasn't affected your courage."

Robert looked at William. William was gazing at the ceiling as if lost in thought. His face wore that expression of shining innocence that his family never saw without a sinking of their hearts.

Robert's mind went back over the evening. It was simply chock-full of mysteries—beginning, now that he came to think of it, with the mysterious production of the fancy dress costume. Yes, he must have a word or two of explanation with William. But not now. This was no moment for words of explanation with William.

Someone was holding up a glass and saying:

"Here's to our hero, Robert Brown!"

Loud cheers and strains of "He's a jolly good fellow" rose on all sides.

Robert blinked modestly.

Someone filled up his glass again.

**THE END**

*Too old to join the Outlaws Club?*
*Then you could join ...*

# The Just William Society

In 1983 a group of Just William enthusiasts met to discuss the work of Richmal Crompton. Since then there has been a William meeting each year. In 1995 a Just William Society was formed.

Richmal Crompton was one of the finest humorous writers of the twentieth century, and the aim of the society is to promote her work – particularly anything connected with Just William. The society currently produces two magazines each year with articles on various William-related topics, as well as holding the annual meeting.

Details of the next meeting and information on membership of the society can be obtained by sending an s.a.e. to:

Public Relations/Events Co-ordinator
The Just William Society
18 Colthill Crescent
Milltimber
Aberdeen AB13 0EG

Richmal Crompton
**Just William at School**

*"School's not nat'ral at all," said William. "Still, I don't*
*suppose they'd let us give it up altogether, 'cause of*
*schoolmasters havin' to have somethin' to do."*

School is fertile ground for a boy of William's infinite trouble-
making talent. Especially when he'd rather not be there at
all. Whether he's feigning illness to avoid a test, campaigning
for the abolition of Latin and Arithmetic, or breaking into Ole
Fathead's house in pursuit of justice, William brings muddle
and mayhem to anyone who tries to teach him a lesson.

Ten classic stories of William at school – and trying
desperately to get out of it!

Richmal Crompton
**Just William on Holiday**

*"No one stops them enjoying themselves,"* muttered William.
*"They go about havin' a good time all the time, but the
minute I start they all get mad at me!"*

Holidays are supposed to be a time for rest and recreation.
But somehow none of the Brown family seem to spend
much time relaxing with William around!

Whether he's rescuing a damsel in distress, sailing the high
seas to discover an uncharted island, or capturing a
dangerous smuggler on the beach, William never fails to turn
his holidays into chaotic adventures that no one will *ever*
forget.

# A selected list of JUST WILLIAM titles available from Macmillan

The prices shown below are correct at the time of going to press. However, Macmillan Publishers reserve the right to show new retail prices on covers which may differ from those previously advertised.

| | | |
|---|---|---|
| Just – William | Richmal Crompton | £3.99 |
| More – William | Richmal Crompton | £3.99 |
| William Again | Richmal Crompton | £3.99 |
| Just William – As Seen on TV | Richmal Crompton | £3.99 |
| William at War | Richmal Crompton | £3.99 |
| Just William at Christmas | Richmal Crompton | £3.99 |
| Just William on Holiday | Richmal Crompton | £3.99 |
| Just William at School | Richmal Crompton | £3.99 |

All *Just William* titles can be ordered at your local bookshop or are available by post from:

**Book Service by Post
PO Box 29, Douglas, Isle of Man IM99 1BQ**

Credit cards accepted. For details:
Telephone: 01624 675137
Fax: 01624 670923
E-mail: bookshop@enterprise.net

**Free postage and packing in the UK.**
Overseas customers: add £1 per book (paperback)
and £3 per book (hardback).